"I'm Zach McCade. Does that name ring a bell?"

The woman studied him and shook her head. "No. Do I know you?"

"Why did you think I had the right to look you over so closely when I first came in?"

The woman flushed. "I—I thought...that maybe you were my...husband or...something."

Zach jerked physically, his mouth dropping slightly before he regained control. "Your... What type of game are you playing, lady?" Zach stood up, grabbing his hat.

Agitated, the woman shook her head. "No. No. You don't understand. Oh, heavens, I—I..."

Zach realized the woman was in real distress, and he moved back to her. "You what, honey?" he said softly, a frown pulling the corners of his lips down. "Just spit it out," he encouraged.

"I—I don't even know who I am!"

Zach gaped as, after that announcement, the woman promptly burst into tears.

Books by Cheryl Wolverton

Love Inspired

A Matter of Trust #11
A Father's Love #20
This Side of Paradise #38
The Best Christmas Ever #47
A Mother's Love #63
For Love of Zach #76

CHERYL WOLVERTON

Growing up in a small military town in Oklahoma, where she used to make up stories with her next-door neighbor, Cheryl says she's always written, but never dreamed of having anything published. But after years of writing her own Sunday school material in the different churches where she's taught young children, and wanting to see more happy endings, she decided to give it a try, and found herself unable to stop.

Seeing so many people hurting, afraid to reach out and accept God's forgiveness, she felt inspired to begin writing romances about God's love and forgiveness, because, she says, "We can't truly have happily ever after if we don't have that happily-ever-after relationship with God, too."

Cheryl now lives in a small Louisiana town and has been happily married for seventeen years. She has two wonderful children who think it's cool to have a "writing mama." Cheryl loves to hear from her readers. You can write to her at P.O. Box 207, Slaughter, LA 70777.

For Love of Zach
Cheryl Wolverton

♥ Love Inspired®

Published by Steeple Hill Books™

STEEPLE HILL BOOKS

Steeple
Hill™

ISBN 0-373-87076-0

FOR LOVE OF ZACH

Copyright © 1999 by Cheryl Wolverton

Visit us at www.steeplehill.com

Printed in U.S.A.

...Forgetting what is behind and straining toward what is ahead, I press on toward the goal to win the prize for which God has called me heavenward in Christ Jesus.

—Philippians 3:13-14

Goodness. There are so many people who helped keep me sane during this book!

Jacqueline Lichtenberg and Jean Lorrah of the Sime~Gen universe who kept bouncing off my hardheaded writing rules. Cherri, who would giggle when I called and say, "Now how many pages have you done today?" Then there is a very new and dear friend whom I can't imagine having not known my entire life—Marge Robbins, my Sosectu, who put up with my moodiness when I couldn't, for the life of me, understand why any sane person would write (okay, it has been pointed out I'm not sane).

A special thank-you to Karen Litman.

And Denise Gray—who has done so much for me in Zachary, Louisiana, to help me promote my book.

As always, to Steve, Christina and Jeremiah. I love you guys. Boy, have you really learned to cook well!

Thanks to my dear friends and family for your love and support. You'll never know how much it means.

Prologue

Laura Walker drove down the deserted highway, almost to her destination. According to a man in the town about an hour and a half back, Hill Creek, Texas was just around the bend. Laura shook her head, not quite sure what the man had meant, but trusting him when he said she'd be there before midnight. He'd even gone in and called the sheriff's office of Hill Creek to find out if there was a hotel available for her while she was there.

Texas hospitality was certainly obvious the farther west she'd gone. Now, here she was, nearly to her destination and she had to wonder just how hospitable Hill Creek was going

to be when she started questioning one of
their prominent citizens about the possibility
of foul play.

A large rain drop splattered on Laura's
windshield, and she sighed in dismay. Turning on the wipers, she looked ahead to where
the headlights cut through the darkness.

Empty, bleak land stretched out from the
long straight highway into the darkness beyond. Absently, Laura reached up and
touched the heart around her neck, wondering
what Mark had seen in this place out here,
just why he'd been out here, and just who he
was running from.

The frantic call telling her he'd discovered
something and was in trouble, but not to
worry, had, of course, had just the opposite
effect Mark had wanted. All her instincts had
been put on alert. And since she was on medical leave, she had the time to investigate.
Guilt ate at her as she thought again how she
had neglected her brother. But her job had
always come first. She had to be a success,
had to prove to her father she could be the
best detective on the force, that she could do
what he had never believed she could up until
the day he died. That she could be the best

big-city detective back where she had been born and raised. Mark understood that. She knew that. But still, if Mark was dead, she didn't know if she would ever be able to forgive herself.

"Father, please help me find the answers. Help me find out what is going on. What he was up to? What was—"

Headlights flashed bright out of the darkness just ahead to her left, startling her. In a blink, a truck shot across the land.

Laura tensed, grabbing the wheel and hitting the brake.

The vehicle barreled straight toward her.

Laura screamed, wrenching the steering wheel.

Impact.

Metal screeched.

Pain exploded.

The world tipped and tilted. Laura felt the seat belt grip and hold as the car twisted and turned.

Her world narrowed to one of pain, confusion and the sound of crunching metal as the car, now on its hood, skidded.

I'm going to die, she thought, despairingly.

I'm going to die and never find out who is after my brother....

The car came to an abrupt halt, tossing Laura against the door.

Her mind spun.

Groggily, Laura realized she must have hit a tree. Reaching toward her waist, she painfully released her seat belt.

Pain burst as she connected with the roof of the car, falling awkwardly from where the seat belt had held her so secure. Black spots appeared before her eyes. Everything went dark. A roaring filled her ears. Realizing she was losing consciousness she fought, slowly, second by second to stay awake. She wasn't sure how long she lay there before the world finally started to right itself. When she did come to, she lay still trying to figure out if anything was broken.

One arm hurt and was almost numb, she realized. Her head was spinning and her entire back and hips hurt. As a matter of fact, taking inventory, she wasn't sure there wasn't a place on her that didn't hurt.

Laura blinked when she realized she was staring at a shoe, a shoe that had been on her foot when she'd been hit.

Giddily, Laura realized she was lucky to be alive.

"Slowly... Move, slowly...." She wiped at her forehead and realized she was covered in blood. Laura simply stared at it, unable to believe this. "I'm bleeding." Absently she brought her hand toward her nose and sniffed the metallic smell.

It was blood. But she smelled something else, too. Sniffing again, she realized she smelled fuel.

A sudden whoosh drew her bleary gaze to the hood of her car. Fire leapt up. Fire... And she was certain she saw booted feet. Hope filled her as she saw someone was there.

"Help!" she cried out, but found her voice so weak she was certain he didn't hear her.

Then the figure bent and looked in. Relieved, she smiled, until she saw the gun.

"Oh, Father," she whispered, just before darkness descended.

Chapter One

The ringing of the phone woke him.

Groggily rolling over, Zach McCade snagged the phone and pulled it over to his ear. "'Lo?"

"Zach? It's Mitch." Zach instantly recognized the low tones of his brother. "I thought you'd like to know the lady with your name in her pocket is coming around. You might want to be here when she wakes up."

Zach pushed up in bed, rubbing at his eyes. "When did this happen?"

"I just got the call from the nurses' station."

"Thanks, little bro, I appreciate it."

"Zach?"

Zach paused, halfway out of bed, the phone already heading toward its cradle. "Yeah?"

"Go easy on her. She's been unconscious over a week. Give her time to explain. I'll be there as soon as I can."

"Of course."

Zach hung up the phone. Going over to his closet, he quickly found a pair of jeans and a button-down shirt Slipping into them, he pulled on a pair of socks, jerked on his boots. Going into the bathroom, he washed his face, brushed his teeth and combed back his hair.

On his way out to his truck, he snagged his hat. The sky was inky black with thousands of small pinpricks of light in it, just like when he'd gotten the call over a week ago asking him to come identify a Jane Doe who'd come into the hospital; or rather, a Laura Doe. According to the doctor, she'd had on a necklace with the name *Laura* on it.

He didn't know anyone named Laura. Perhaps it was one of the people coming to interview as the new housekeeper out at his place. So, he'd gone in to check on her.

Remembering the swelling of her face and

all the bandages, he didn't think he could have identified her even if he'd known her.

Turning the truck around, he shot up the long driveway toward the main highway leading to Hill Creek. At this time of night no other headlights could be seen. Very few people were up after dark. Most of the ranchers out here kept rancher's hours, up before dawn and in bed right after dark.

Zach was no different. On the occasion he was up after dark, it was to visit one of his brothers, or to run his daughter somewhere. At fifteen, almost sixteen, she liked to spend the night with all of her friends, but couldn't drive there by herself yet.

That was where she was tonight—at a friend's. Which benefited him in this case. He sure missed her when she was gone.

Zach sighed.

At thirty-six, Zach felt he had seen everything there was to see in life. Losing his wife like he had, having to raise a daughter on his own——and before that raising his two younger brothers after their parents had died, had taught him some hard lessons.

It was a miracle from God that they hadn't lost the ranch. At nineteen and having the entire world collapse out from under him had not been a normal child's dream. Even meeting his wife...

She hadn't been happy with a normal job.

She had paid for it with her life, leaving a preadolescent child behind.

Still, he took his responsibilities seriously. That's why he was driving into town now. He wanted to find out who this woman was, solve the problem of just why she had his name in her pocket. Then, perhaps, he could get on with raising his daughter.

Zach rubbed at his neck, thinking of Angela. She was so headstrong. He didn't need this woman to worry about right now. He needed a full-time cook, someone who was there for Angela when he couldn't be; a...companion.

He didn't dare call the help a *baby-sitter*. His daughter would hit the roof. But he needed someone, a woman who could influence Angela, perhaps give pointers on *women things*. Things he didn't know how to talk to her about.

"God, I need a housekeeper. Someone who can take a hand and help me with Angela. Please let this woman be one of the interviewees. Not like the last one, who drank, or the one before that, who only had marriage to some rich rancher on her mind, or like the woman who kept falling asleep through the entire interview. Please let this woman have some common sense and actually like kids.''

Zach thought of the one woman who had made it more than clear she hated kids—a former rodeo rider. Zach shuddered. Surely good help shouldn't be that hard to find. And he had to find someone before the school ball. He had promised himself that his daughter wouldn't be embarrassed again. And a woman was just the thing Angela needed to teach her the soft side before the ball.

Which brought his mind back to the woman named Laura, the possible inter-viewee who had been run off the road. He would talk to her, find out if that was why she'd had his name in her pocket, though he could think of nothing else.

Zach turned into the parking lot of the local hospital and parked the truck. Getting out, he quickly made his way through the sterile halls of the hospital to the wing where Laura Doe was being kept.

''Zach!''

Zach glanced about in surprise to see his brother coming in a side door. "You got here fast, Mitch. What'd you do? Speed?"

"Nah. Mrs. Culpepper was seeing ghosts out back of her house again and I had to go and check it out. So I wasn't at my house."

"Haven't had a chance to talk to Laura Doe yet, then?"

Mitch shook his head. Holding his cowboy hat in his hand he looked up at Zach. "We still haven't found the person who hit her."

"Someone drunk, most probably, passing through the county."

Mitch sighed. "I sure hope the woman can give us some idea. I'd like to catch who did this. The entire side of her car was caved in. Whoever hit her had to have been driving fast."

Zach sighed as he turned toward the door. "At least Will saw the fire and happened to find her. She would have ended up dead otherwise."

Zach started to push the door open, but Mitch stopped him with a hand on his arm. "Would you rather me question her, Zach? I mean, if this reminds you too much of Carolyn..."

Anguish clutched at Zach. Memories of the last time he'd been in a hospital room assailed him. The pain, the sense of loss as he had sat by his wife's side, of her never regaining consciousness.

Forcing the pain aside, Zach shook his head. "She had my name on her. I'll talk to her."

"You're not responsible for this woman, Zach. Don't—"

Zach shot Mitch a firm look. "I'll handle it."

Zach walked into the dimly lit room and paused, searching through the shadows. Miniblinds covered the windows and a water pitcher sat on a small table next to the bed. Two chairs for visitors filled up the empty space. A TV was protruding from the wall next to another door that led to a rest room.

An IV machine beeped as the fluid bag, almost empty, ran into the patient's arm. Following that small tube, which had been giving the patient fluids for the past week, he studied where it went into her hand. The hand was a dainty hand, long graceful fingers, though the nails were short and clean.

Her arm rested gently across the top sheet

over her abdomen. She hardly made a dent in the large bed. He hadn't realized she was that small before. Moving his gaze up he traced her body until he reached her face…and met beautiful blue eyes.

A smile curved her lips.

Zach found himself flushing even as he noticed her bruises were mostly gone now. He cleared his throat. "I, um, apologize for staring."

Confusion crossed her face. He watched as the blond-haired woman swept her gaze over him very thoroughly. Finally, she lifted her eyes back to his and he saw uncertainty in them. "I thought you had the right…"

"I just heard the Jane Doe is awake and thought I'd come check…"

Distracted from what the woman said, Zach looked around to see Deputy Harry Colchester coming through the door.

Mitch, who was leaning against the wall nearby—Zach hadn't even realized his brother had come in—straightened. "Harry, what are you doing here?"

The man paused, his dark eyes sweeping the room. "Hi, boss. I was checking out someone at the hospital, and rumor reached me that she was awake. I was coming to question her. What's your brother doing here?''

Zach nodded at Harry. "I was talking with the woman. Nice to see you again, Harry."

Mitch waved Harry on in, over to his side.

"You were talking with her? You know this woman and didn't tell us?"

Zach frowned at the obvious shock in Harry's voice. Before he could say anything, Mitch motioned Harry to silence. "No one knows her, Harry. But she had my brother's name in her pocket. There was always the chance..."

"No one knows me?"

The soft trembling voice drew all their attention to the bed. Zach unconsciously moved forward when he realized how pale the woman had turned. "It's all right, Miss... Laura, I'm sure that when you tell us who you are, we'll find whoever you were coming to visit."

Zach wondered if the shock of seeing so many people in the room at once had rattled her. "You had my name in your pocket—"

"You know my name!"

Zach moved forward again. Tossing his hat on the small bedside table, he reached out and took the woman's hand. "You were uncon-scious when you came in ma'am. The neck-lace they found around your neck said Laura on it."

Her small hand gripped his firmly. He won-dered if she was trying to draw strength from him and said a soft prayer of peace for her as she adjusted to her surroundings. "Your car was burned beyond recognition. It was lucky Will found you and got you out or you'd be dead now."

"Zach!"

His brother's voice pulled his gaze around to see the warning in Mitch's eyes.

"I...my car. I don't...understand."

Guilt assailed Zach as he realized his blunt words had confused her even more. Sighing, he apologized. "I'm sorry for that, ma'am."

Mitch interrupted. "If you could just tell us, perhaps, why you were driving here to-ward Hill Creek, with my brother's name in your pocket?"

"Probably the job, Mitch," Harry sug-gested.

"Job?" Large blue eyes went from Mitch, to Harry, then landed back on him. It felt like a punch to the gut as she looked at him so helplessly. "Please...explain."

The distress in the small woman's voice told Zach something wasn't right here. Sitting down on the edge of the bed, he studied her. "Give me a minute, Mitch," he said over his shoulder.

"Sure, Zach."

"You shouldn't let him do this—" Harry protested.

"He's my brother, Harry. I trust him. Now get." Mitch herded Harry out the door, pulling it closed behind him.

"Just calm down, Miss Laura. Everything is going to be fine."

Banked panic in her eyes worried him. Unconsciously he squeezed her hand and leaned forward, keeping eye contact. Softly, he murmured, "Just relax and we'll take this one thing at a time. Okay? One step at time."

Slowly the panic subsided.

Finally, she nodded jerkily. Zach allowed a smile to stretch his lips. *Father, guide me in the questioning. Show me what to do.*

Laura's first words came back to him and he decided there was the place to start. "I'm Zach McCade. Does that name ring a bell?"

The woman studied him and shook her head. "No. I— Do I know you?"

"Why did you think I had the right to look you over so closely when I first came in?"

The woman flushed.

Zach couldn't blame her. He felt his cheeks heat up at getting caught looking a woman over like that. He had no idea what had gotten into him except he'd allowed his curiosity to get the best of him

"I—I—I thought..."

"Yes?"

Her gaze slid away. "...that maybe you were my...husband or...something."

Zach jerked physically, his mouth dropping slightly before regaining control. "Your... What type of game are you playing, lady?" Zach released her hand and stood up, grabbing his hat.

"I'm not playing any game." The woman's cry of distress got to Zach, calming him, making him regret his outburst. He hated seeing a woman upset. But he didn't like games like this, either.

"Then how about you tell me just what you're doing out here and why you had my name and address in your pocket?"

"I don't know!"

Zach shook his head, thoroughly confused. "Fine. Take it up with my brother."

He turned toward the door.

"Please...don't leave me. I—I—I'm scared."

Zach gritted his teeth and turned around. "Tell me your last name. Tell me why you're here. And tell me just what you thought you could gain by pulling such a stunt."

"I don't know. I—I don't know."

Zach shook his head. "Look, lady. I don't want any problems, either. We can just chalk this up to confusion or something. Really. Why don't you let me call someone? You do have relatives—somewhere?"

The woman shook her head agitated. "No. No. You don't understand. I don't know. I—I thought you understood. Oh, heavens, I—I—"

Zach realized the woman was in real distress, not playing games and moved back toward her. "You what, honey?" he said in a softer voice, a frown pulling the corners of his lips down. "Just spit it out," he encouraged.

When she simply stared at him, he added

softly, "I'm sorry I wasn't very understanding earlier."

Zach wondered if in those first few moments of consciousness she had mistaken him for a loved one. He reached out to stroke her arm reassuringly.

"I don't know if I do or not. I—I don't even know who I am!"

Zach gaped as the woman, after that announcement, promptly burst into tears.

Chapter Two

She felt like a total fool, sobbing while this strange man loomed over her, gaping at her like a fish out of water.

"Have you never seen a woman cry before?" she snapped at him, humiliated. Whoever she was, she was certain she didn't like people seeing her like this.

The man moved forward and sat down on the bed and reached for her, pulling her forward into his arms. Though she was still sore and bruised from the accident, the doctor had said nothing was broken. He hadn't told her anything else except that her memory would come back probably when she saw someone she knew, and then he'd left. How was she to know the person he called wasn't related?

Strong warmth enveloped her as the man held her close and tried to shush her. A spicy cologne drifted to her nose, unfamiliar in its scent. "What cologne are you wearing?" she asked, hiccuping as she forced her tears aside.

"My cologne?"

Laura realized what a silly question that must be to him. "It doesn't matter. It doesn't smell familiar. Even if it did, I probably wouldn't know, would I?"

"Now, there, there...miss...ma'am...Laura. Just relax. We'll figure this out."

The soft low murmurs ran through her, reassuring her.

"I feel so alone, so empty, Mr. McCade."

"It's Zach. And Laura, the Bible tells us the Lord will never leave us or forsake us."

Peace flooded Laura, and she knew she'd heard those words before. "That's right," she whispered.

She shuddered and finally rested against him. He eased her back, looking down into her eyes with concern. "You know that?"

Gazing into his brown eyes she thought they were the eyes of a man who took responsibility seriously. He had a firm jaw, covered with a day's growth of beard, which only made him look more rugged. The curl of hair over his forehead made him almost boyish. She wanted to touch it, but instead, reached up to touch her own hair. She felt the gauze that still wrapped her head where she had evidently banged herself. "I think so. The words are there, in my heart. Familiar. The doctor said this—" she indicated the bandage "—probably took part of my memory and it'd come back when I saw something or someone familiar."

Zach reached up and cupped her cheek. "It'll be okay."

Laura shook her head, feeling the rough calluses on his fingers brush her temple and jaw. She liked the comfort, the reassurance his hand offered in that one touch, but still, said, "I don't know. You said I was in a wreck. I don't even remember that."

Zach sighed and moved back from her.

She immediately missed his warmth.

Zach ran a hand down his face and then

around to his neck and rubbed it. Shaking his head, he sighed. "I don't know if I should say anything. I mean, in cases like this, aren't you not supposed to say anything so the person who can't remember can figure it out on her own?"

"No! Please!"

A nurse came in to change the IV bag, and Zach moved out of her way. Laura didn't want him moving away. She wanted him there, by her, closer. As the nurse left she saw the two police officers standing out in the hall, talking. Nervousness assailed her. She wondered if she had done something criminal before she'd lost her memory. "Please, Mr.—Zach. Please, Zach. I want to remember. It's—horrible not able to remember anything. It's like a big black nothing. Please help me."

Indecision crossed his face before he nodded. "From what I understand, you were on your way into town out on the highway, when you were evidently sideswiped by a drunk or something. Your car caught fire. Will Whitefeather, an old hermit who lives out in the desert, found you and dragged you out of the car. He sat with you until someone came by to help."

"And?" she asked when he stopped.

"I'm afraid that's it. The car was burned beyond recognition, and the only thing you had on you was your necklace and a piece of paper with my name and address on it."

"Then I know you?" she asked, frustration and confusion warring in her and bringing on a headache.

Zach shook his head. "No ma'am. I'm afraid I've never met you in my life."

Despair swamped her. "Then what was I doing with your name?"

Frowning, Zach rubbed his chin. "As close as I can tell, you were perhaps on your way out to interview for the job that I advertised."

Helplessly, Laura shook her head. "What job is that?"

"Housekeeper. Actually, light housekeeping and assisting my daughter with the chores around the ranch that she does. And just being there when she needs...well, when she needs a woman to talk about girl things."

Laura watched as the man actually reddened. "Ah, child care," she said, a small smile curving her mouth as she temporarily forgot her problems in the light of this man's insecurities.

He looked up with a boyish look on his face. "Not at all, ma'am. I just want my daughter to have some womanly company."

She wanted to ask about his wife. Obviously, there was no woman around. Feeling that wasn't her business, she let it drop. When she did, her own problems flooded back in her. A small voice came up out of the dark mists. *Lean not unto your own understandings.*

Her gaze jerked to Zach's. "I remember…a…verse. 'Lean not unto your own understandings.' Why would I remember that?"

Laura was amazed and excited to remember something.

"Perhaps because you need those words of wisdom right now."

"Let me see if I can remember…." Laura concentrated and tried to think. "Evidently I like to read my Bible, because I can remember other verses…."

Lifting a hand, she rubbed at her head as the headache intensified.

"Don't push it, Laura." The deep soft tones reached her through the pain, and she looked up.

"I want to know, though."

Concern shone bright in his eyes. "I know you do. But right now you need to concentrate on rest and getting well. Your memory will come back, in time."

"Are you sure?" She knew, even as she asked the question, it wasn't a fair one. "I'm sorry. No one is sure." Laura rubbed at her eyes, which were getting tired. "What am I going to do when I'm well and ready to leave the hospital if my memory hasn't returned? You said I know no one. Is it possible someone will be looking for me?"

Zach picked up his hat and slapped it absently against his leg. "Don't worry, Laura. You'll have a place with my daughter and me until your memory returns."

Laura glanced up at Zach, stunned. "But you don't even know me," she whispered.

Zach shrugged. "You were coming here to apply for the job. That's close enough for me. Besides, out here we take care of each other. Now, lie back and get some rest. You look like you're about to fall over with exhaustion. We'll talk tomorrow.''

She nodded, feeling exactly like what he'd said. Just the short conversation and all of the emotions had physically and emotionally exhausted her. Surprisingly, no matter how worried she was, there was a lingering peace at remembering something and she was certain she could sleep.

Looking up, she smiled softly at the kind man. ''Thank you, Zach, for your help.''

He returned the smile. ''Sleep.''

Her eyes slowly drifted closed.

Zach waited until her eyes were shut and she was breathing regularly before backing out of the room.

''How is she?''

Zach turned to face Mitch, noting Harry was gone. ''She's sleeping. She has amnesia, Mitch.''

Mitch gaped, then laughed. ''Sure. Tell me another one.''

''I'm serious.''

Mitch studied his older brother.

Zach simply stared.

"But that's not real. That only happens in stories and...and..."

"And movies. I know. But she couldn't have faked what happened in there. I thought she was pulling my leg and threatened her with fraud. She wasn't lying, Mitch. Take my word for it."

Mitch sighed before slipping his hat on his head. "This is just great. Could she tell you anything?"

Zach smiled slightly. "She knows her memory verses."

"What?"

Zach chuckled. "Surprised me and her both when she popped up with one. As a matter of fact, she was so excited about remembering it that she started trying to remember others and from the looks of it, stirred up quite a headache."

"So, it looks like we'll just have to wait until she's better to talk with her? That's a shame. I would have liked to close this file. I don't like people doing things like this in my county."

Zach smiled at his younger brother. At one time he'd been afraid it would be the sheriff who arrested his little brother. Instead, the sheriff had taken Mitch under his wing and today Mitch was the youngest sheriff Hill Creek had ever elected. To hear his brother say something like that made Zach proud. "Well, it looks like it *is* closed. Some drunk hit her and our patient in there was simply on her way to apply for a job. By the way, I told her she could stay out at the ranch until she gets her memory back."

Mitch frowned. "Is that a good idea?"

Zach sighed. "She'll get the small housekeeper's room."

"You're going to make her work?" Mitch asked, shocked.

"Of course not. But, since she was coming to apply for the job, what better way to see if it'll work out? In the time she's there I'll have a chance to watch and assess her, like a trial period, with Angela. See how things go."

Mitch grinned at his brother. "In other words, Angela won't realize this woman might be the woman who has been brought in to *stifle* her, I believe is how she put it?"

Zach slipped his hat onto his head. "That's

about it. I'm off to home. Call me when they get ready to dismiss her. I have a lot of work that needs to get done, and in just a few hours, too. I'd like to get another hour or two of sleep first.''

Mitch nodded. "I'll hunt down that doctor and get a more thorough report from him. If he can't tell me what I want to know, then we'll get our little brother to look at her.''

"You do that.'' Zach headed down the hall. As he walked, the confused, fearful bright blue eyes of Laura Doe haunted him. "So, Father, what do you have in store for that woman? Why'd you take her memory? And why did you send someone so pretty my way?''

Shaking his head in disgust at his thoughts, he pushed open the door and headed out toward his truck, reminding himself this woman had no memory and she was only his responsibility, that was all. Nothing would happen. Nothing at all.

Chapter Three

Had he really thought this woman was safe? Zach stared in disbelief at his entire coop of chickens running loose in his front yard.

"She insisted on seeing the chickens."

Harry's amused voice came from near the barn. Zach turned from his station at the front door of the porch to look at the deputy sheriff.

Two of his ranch hands stood with Harry. "I was just getting some hands to help gather the animals up."

He looked from Harry back to the woman who was waving her hands at the chickens and only upsetting them further. He stared at her.

The bandage around her head had been replaced with a patch over the wound. Her hair was pulled back with a blue ribbon at her neck. The new blue jeans and powder-blue shirt fit perfectly. He nodded with approval. The general store had done an excellent job of judging her size. Her hands were pink and still shiny-looking. It'd be a couple of weeks before he could run her in and let Mitch do a fingerprinting. Of course, with the way her hands were burned, they weren't likely to find a good match. Mitch had a bulletin out on her now. The way she was chasing down his chickens made him think she was doing really well and would probably get her memory back at any time.

"Why didn't you call me, Harry? I'd have come and picked her up."

Laura turned from where she was trying to gather up the chickens, exasperation on her face. "I thought chickens enjoyed their coops. These things took flight the minute I walked in."

Zach chuckled and moved down the stairs from the porch. "Angela. Come out and meet our company," he called over his shoulder.

"Actually, Laura," Zach said smiling and going over to take her elbow, "why not just let Red and the others handle this? You come on in out of the sun."

Laura looked at him in disbelief. "I'm not fragile."

He smiled. "I'd feel better, since you're just out of the hospital, okay? And I'd like you to meet my daughter."

As if on cue, the door flew open and a very lovely girl bounced out onto the porch. She stopped at the edge of the steps. "Afternoon, Miss Laura." Her gaze hopped to his. "Can I go to Bebe's now?"

"I want you here, Angela. Perhaps tomorrow."

"Aww, dad!" Angela spun and stormed back into the house.

Zach sighed.

Laura looked from the pert little woman-child to the father, still feeling in a whirlwind. "That's who you need child care for?"

Shaking his head, Zach resumed leading her up the steps toward the door. "No. A companion, though she doesn't know that. A friend. Call it what you will. She's trying her wings right now. Sorry about her abrupt departure. It's spring, and she has a lot of chores she's in charge of. She'd like to get out of them, if possible."

Zach smiled at her and Laura's heart smiled with him. His smile made her feel good, and she reveled in it.

"And she doesn't like that?"

"There's not a lot of people out here for her to talk to. It's only natural she'd want to be around her friends."

Laura nodded. "I see. Does she know about my...condition?"

"I thought it best if I talked to you first before telling her. I wasn't sure if you'd mind people knowing."

Laura shrugged. "I don't have much choice, do I? I mean, if they ask me who I am then I'm sure they're going to wonder why I can't tell them a last name."

Zach nodded and escorted Laura into the living room. "Here we are."

Old and country came to mind as Laura glanced at the quaint living room. Pictures of short, squat trees and horses and Native Americans that decorated the walls broke up the starkness of the white paint. The waxed wooden floor covered with the occasional throw rug shone brightly. But the furniture—plush and comfortable in earth tones—really set off the dark look of the room adding a lightness, a homey feel. Magazines and newspapers were near a big overstuffed rocker.

Laura didn't see any signs of a woman's touch, no pastel borders along the wall, or lacy little doilies or floral arrangements.

"Nice," she murmured softly. "Pleasant."

"Well, it's not much, but it's home," Zach said moving up next to her. His deep, low tones were comforting, reassuring.

"Home is where the heart is, they say," Laura said and smiled.

"It's just plain curious how you can remember some things and not others," Zach stated, studying her curiously.

Laura stared into the compassionate eyes, sinking into the welcoming warmth. "Yeah. I can tell you we passed a silver leaf maple out there. But how I know, if I've ever seen one before—" she shrugged, helplessly "—I can't tell you."

She frowned, dark feelings settling down upon her, closing in, suffocating her.

"Let's not think about that right now," Zach murmured and lifted her hand.

Her gaze focused on his strong, darkly tanned fingers as he held her pink, healing ones. She watched him turn her hand and trace the place where there had been some second- and third-degree burns. "They said I must have been pulling myself out of the car to do this. I wish I could thank Mr. White-feather for rescuing me."

Zach stroked her hand again. "Will's a hermit. I doubt you'll see him. He doesn't come around often. Pretty much keeps to himself. Good man, though."

"And, I'd like to thank you for taking me in like this."

The sounds of the door opening drew their gazes to Harry.

"Here you go, ma'am. The outfits the store sent over."

Laura smiled her thanks at Harry. "Thank you so much for the ride, Harry."

"No problem."

Zach moved forward, taking the sack from him. "Tell Mitch I'll call him later."

Harry nodded, then reseated his hat more firmly on his head. "Will do. And if you remember anything, Miss Laura, you be sure and call me immediately. You hear?"

"I hear," Laura replied, smiling at how quaint that sounded.

Zach walked him to the door and then turned. "Well."

Laura heard the quiet interrupted only by the sounds of Angela's voice down the hall. A door slammed, the engine started, and then they heard the sound of a truck pulling away. "Thank you," Laura said.

Her words galvanized Zach. "Why don't I show you where you can stay while you're here?"

"That'd be nice."

Lifting a hand, he gestured down the hallway. "It's down here in the back."

Laura moved forward and followed Zach down the hall. "This is a nice house, Zach."

"It belonged to my parents, and their parents before them."

"But were the walls painted white with the

nice woodwork?'' she asked, admiring the work done in the hall.

''No. Angela's mom had that done.'' Zach paused by a room. ''This here is the study and—'' moving on across the hall, he pointed into a brightly lit room, the large windows giving the room an airy feeling ''—this is the den.''

Laura saw the young girl she'd met earlier sitting on a sofa and talking on the phone.

''Angela. You need to get supper started.''

Angela looked at her father before mumbling something into the phone and hanging it up. ''I was on the phone.''

''I saw that. Now, go get something out to thaw for supper. You can talk later.''

Angela's mouth turned mulish as she strode out of the room and down the hall.

Zach turned and started on down the hall. ''And here are the bedrooms to the right.''

''Is she going to be okay?''

Zach paused in front of a room. Laura could see pink ruffles everywhere and gathered this must be Angela's room. She watched as Zach's shoulders drooped momentarily. Finally he turned to face her.

"Angela and I don't see eye to eye. I don't know...she sits on the phone all day, resents anything I ask." Zach shook his head. "I just don't know how to communicate with her right now."

Zach continued down the hall, passing two more rooms before stepping into the third one and placing the sack on the bed. "I sure wish her mama were here at times like this. Because I can tell you, I sure feel inadequate."

Laura's heart went out to the man standing before her. "It's times like that you just have to hold on to God's hand."

Zach turned. "Isn't that the truth. It's been many nights I've spent on my knees over that child. No one ever realizes, until they have children, just how precious they are...and then some still don't."

Laura saw a dark cloud fill his eyes. "Your wife?"

Zach glanced up, surprised. "Yeah. Well," he said, rubbing his hands down his jeans, "enough of my bellyaching. The bathroom is across the hall. Feel free to make yourself at home. We have TV, some books in the den. Angela reads, too, and has a whole stockpile of books in her room. If you want something else, feel free to ask. Oh, and be careful about wandering around outside. It's easy to get lost, plus we have snakes bad this year.''

Laura nodded. "Snakes."

The seriousness melted from Zach's face and a small grin replaced it. "You afraid of snakes?"

"I don't think so. I don't feel any fear."

Zach moved toward her and slipped an arm around her giving her a brief hug. "I'm sorry, Laura. I didn't think when I asked that. You'll remember in time."

Laura couldn't resist slipping her arms around the man and hugging him back. The contact felt good. And, she realized as she hugged him, he felt good; strong, firm, sturdy. She felt unexplained tears fill her eyes and quickly pulled back.

"Thank you, Zach," she said, avoiding his gaze.

Zach touched her chin, tilting her head up. He studied her face for a moment, compassion in his eyes. "You are going to remember, Laura. We'll find out who you are soon. You just hang in there."

Laura attempted a smile. "And you hang in there with your daughter. You're going to reach through to her."

Zach nodded. "I have to get back to work. I'll see you this evening."

"I'll be here."

Laura watched him walk out, the masculine musky scent lingering.

Turning, she crossed to the bed and seated herself on the white, crocheted bedspread. Smoothing a hand over it, she whispered, "Thank you, God, for this family and a place to stay."

Looking up at the ceiling, she whispered, "How come I have such a desire to help Angela? I can't even remember my own life, but my heart is aching for her and the wall between the two of them. I don't even know them, Father."

Smiling she walked over to the window and looked out. "But I know enough to know they're nice people. Thank You for bringing them across my path when You did. And Father, help me...my memory. I don't understand why it hasn't come back yet. Please help me remember."

Laura paused, feeling a sweet warm peace fill her. Despite her amnesia, despite the fact that she was in a stranger's house with no one around, despite it all, she felt that she would regain her memory in His time.

"Thank you, Father. I lean on You and trust You over the next few days and will trust Your will to be done in this."

Turning from the window, she decided to explore the house some before a nap. And while she was at it, she'd stop by and meet Angela, without Zach around. Perhaps she'd learn a little more about the girl with just the two of them there.

Chapter Four

"But I want to help. I'm going to go insane just sitting here."

Zach shook his head, totally dumbfounded by the woman's demand to work. "You should still be resting," he countered.

Taking his hat off, he hung it on the coat-rack just inside the door. He hadn't gotten two steps in the house before Laura had said she wanted to talk to him about working.

And he'd made the mistake of telling her she didn't need to.

"I've rested until I'm all rested out. I'm stiff and sore, and the only way I'm going to feel better is to move around and do some work."

Zach studied Laura. The color was back in her cheeks and most of the bruises had completely faded. He wondered about her ribs and one arm. The doctor had told him she had some particularly nasty bruises there. Still, the other visible bruises were gone. And she did seem to be getting around well enough.

Walking over, he reached and carefully lifted one of her delicate hands, examining it. "Are the other burns healed?"

"Yes."

The soft husky sound made Zach again wonder if this woman had ever sung. Her voice was beautiful, deep, low, alto.

Turning her hand over he noted the healing skin. She was going to be scarred, but at least she still had all ten fingers and they were movable. "I'd hate for you to get these infected, Laura."

"I'll be careful. But Zach, I am not used to just sitting around. My body is demanding exercise and release of energy. I'd like to have something to do, especially when I'm here alone."

Zach absently rubbed a thumb over the soft skin of her wrist. "There are things you can do around here, I imagine. Maybe dusting and, I don't know, helping Angela somehow.... Speaking of which, where is she?"

Zach only wanted to change the subject. Realizing he still held her hand, he released it and moved across the room. "Have you remembered anything yet?"

"Not really," Laura said, watching the way Zach's shirt stretched taut across his shoulders when he propped his hands on his hips. Strength and safety. That's what she felt every time she was around him.

"You've remembered something then?" He looked over his shoulder at her.

Laura shook her head. "Only dreams."

Zach turned and strode back over to her. Taking her hand he led her over to the sofa. He sat down, pulling her gently down beside him. "Dreams?"

The quiet encouragement in his voice prompted Laura to add, "They're fuzzy. I'm in a fog, a red haze, and through the haze I hear a laugh and see...the skins of snakes floating toward me."

Zach's brow furrowed. Slowly he shook his head. "The mind is a strange thing. Don't push it, Laura. It'll all come sooner or later."

Laura smiled. "Thanks, Zach."

The sound of voices outside drew their attention to the front yard. "Angela isn't here?" Zach asked, standing.

Laura stood too. "No. She went to a friend's. Took off on her horse right after school."

Zach pushed open the front door, and Laura could see a young boy on a horse just riding off. At the sound of the door, Angela turned, her chin going up in the air belligerently.

"Are your chores done?"

Laura blinked at the short sound in Zach's voice.

"I'm going to do them now," Angela replied in the same short voice before turning her horse and heading to the barn.

Zach's shoulders slumped. "She's not supposed to leave here without my permission."

Laura touched his shoulder. "She told me, Zach, where she was going to be."

Zach stiffened, then relaxed. "I suppose

that's a step in the right direction. She's too young to be riding off with boys and stuff.''

Laura chuckled. "I have a feeling this is a normal daddy-daughter thing. Did you raise her right, Zach?''

Zach turned and looked down at Laura. "I did my best.''

"Then you need to give her some space. She's going to make mistakes. You need to guide her, then step back and let her make those mistakes so you can be there for her when she comes home hurting.''

Zach's jaw hardened. "It's my job to take care of her and see that nothing bad happens to her.''

Laura nodded. "Yes. But sometimes you have to trust God to do that, too.''

Zach shook his head. "I don't know if I can. Not with my daughter.''

Laura put her hand on Zach's arm absently. "Maybe I should go help her.''

"It's not your responsibility.''

Laura chuckled. "Mr. McCade. What did you say you were going to hire me for?''

"But I didn't say I had hired you. I offered you a place to stay.''

"Well, I want to work and it looks like we just hit upon the ideal solution. You can allow me to do the job you were originally looking to fill. I'll do the job while waiting for my memory to return. If I don't work out, fine. But in the meantime you won't have to worry about your daughter being alone or finding someone to help around the house, and it'll give me something to do."

Zach pursed his lips and finally nodded. "It's a deal. I suppose I should find a way to apologize for being so curt just now."

Laura grinned, relieved to have some direction for herself and to see that Zach really did care about his daughter. "Just love her, Zach. That's all any teenage girl wants."

"I do love her. That's for sure."

Laura winked and started out the front door. "Since Angela has avoided me these past two days, I think I'll go get to know her a little better."

"Tell her I'll start supper."

Laura softened. "I bet that'll mean a lot to her, Zach. I'll tell her."

Laura saw uncertainty leave his eyes and determination to do the task appear. Turning, she walked out the door. He loved his daughter, that was certain. She had to wonder what had happened between the two that had caused such a rift. Crossing the yard and dirt drive, she headed toward the barn. Laura nodded to the men she passed as they were coming in and heading home for the day.

Laura found the stables and went inside. They weren't exactly what she had expected. Clean, and all in a nice neat row, they had eight well-kept stalls. Some had horses, others didn't. The one she was interested in, the one where Angela worked over a bay mare, was the last one on the right.

"Hi, there," Laura said walking up to the gate and looking over it.

Angela glanced up, the brush pausing where she made long sweeping gestures over her horse's tummy. "Hello."

"Your horse is beautiful. How old is it?"

Angela smiled. "Three years. Mountain Magic—" Angela motioned to a horse outside running in the field "—that's her father. Her mother died birthing her."

"Can I pet it?"

"How much do you know about horses?" Angela asked, still stroking the horse gently.

Laura chuckled. "I have no idea. How about we find out?"

Angela laid the brush aside. "You really lost your memory, didn't you?"

Laura nodded. "I sure did." Touching her head where the bump was now only an ugly bruise, she shrugged. "It's the oddest thing. Some things I know, like I love strawberries. But if you ask me where I live, I have no idea."

"Wow," Angela said. "Okay, you can pet Jingle Bells, but be careful. Don't startle her."

"Jingle Bells?" Laura's eyes widened with mirth. "Who named your horse?"

A slow smile curved Angela's mouth, transforming the dirty urchin into a beautiful child-woman. "I did. I was only twelve when she was born, though." She moved forward and took hold of the horse's head. "I'm stuck with that name now."

Laura walked into the stall and then paused. "Now what?"

Angela patted the horse's neck, motioning

with her head. "Come on over here and just pat it like I am."

Laura worked her way around the horse, feeling nervousness build. "She's huge."

"Yeah. Don't get nervous. Jingle Bells will sense that. Just move up here and pet her."

Laura got within a foot of the horse and stopped. "I don't think I've been around horses before."

She knew she sounded breathless, but that couldn't be helped. Panic attacks did that, she supposed.

"Miss Laura, you've got to be kidding! You can't be scared of horses. Jingle Bells is an angel."

"Yeah?" Laura looked at the horse, then back at Angela. "Why's it smiling like that at me?"

The horse took that moment to snort and shake its head. "See," Laura said. "Maybe I fell off one when I was a kid or something. Maybe I've never been around them, but I can definitely tell you, I know nothing about horses."

Angela rolled her eyes, then promptly reached out and grabbed Laura by the arm.

"Whoa!" Laura said, but Angela didn't stop. Instead, she slid Laura's hand up the neck of the horse.

"See there, Miss Laura. Jingle Bells isn't going to hurt you. Just move your hand up and down like this." Laura watched Angela as she controlled her hand and moved it up and down the neck, then looked at the horse. Laura wondered if she was supposed to see the whites of the horse's eyes like that. "It's sneering at me."

Angela giggled like a typical teenager and released Laura's hand. Laura didn't immediately pull back since Angela seemed to think this was so important. She continued to stand there with her hand on the horse's neck.

"Horses don't sneer. Now, let me get her some oats and then we can go."

"Hey, wait...um, Angela, don't leave me here." Her voice rose as the girl retreated down the row of stables.

"You'll be fine," she called back, giggling.

Laura turned her gaze back to the horse. "You hear that," she whispered, "I'll be fine."

The horse advanced on her.

Laura took a step back. "Be still you huge beast. See, I'm petting you." *Pat, pat, pat.* "Now just be...youch!"

The horse's foot came down right on hers. She tried to move back, but the monstrosity had her pinned against the wood. "Angela! The...the horse. It's on...my...foot!"

Angela coming down the isle with bucket in hand chuckled. "She isn't on your foot. If she was, it'd be broken. She's just playing with you. Food, Jingle Bells!"

The horse turned and trotted over to the feed area.

Laura wilted in relief.

"You know, Miss Laura, if you're to be on this ranch any time at all, you have to learn how to be around horses and how to ride them."

Laura blinked at the girl, certain she was kidding.

She wasn't kidding. Angela looked earnest and a bit anticipatory and something else....

Laura realized with blinding insight that what else was in Angela's gaze was loneliness. The girl actually wanted the job of teaching her how to ride a horse.

Father, God, You have got to be kidding. I'll break my neck if I try to get on something this big. I mean, yeah, I like Angela and want to help fix the problem here, but...this?

But her heart opened and a gentle sweet thought came to her, *Lean not unto thine own understanding.*

Laura mentally reached out and grabbed on to her Father's hand, holding tightly. *I trust you, Father.*

"Perhaps you're right, Angela. I mean, I really should. Then maybe you could show me this beautiful land out here and we could ride together some."

"All right! You'll love it. I love horses more than anything...well, except for boys." Angela giggled, totally relaxed, her face beaming with joy as she quickly motioned Laura out and latched the gate. "You'll have a blast. Horses are the best things in the world, and one day I'm going to be a horse trainer."

"Great. I can't wait to learn. After all, how hard can it be?"

Chapter Five

Very hard, Laura thought sitting on the ground, pain making her bottom numb.

"No, no, no, Miss Laura, that's not the way."

"Your horse pushed me. My foot would have been fine if she hadn't pushed me."

"Jingle Bells is one of the most docile horses we have. She didn't push you."

"What do you call what it did?"

"You have to learn to control her and then she won't walk off on you."

"Good afternoon, ladies."

Laura groaned. It couldn't be. *Not him. Not now.*

"The ground comfortable there, Miss Laura?"

Laura shifted to look over her shoulder.

Zach stood, boot propped up on a lower rung of the fence, smiling blandly. He was too handsome for words this afternoon, wearing a pullover white shirt and worn jeans that hugged his legs. His brown hair fell over his forehead, wavy and damp with perspiration. His hand hung loosely over the top rung of the fence and his eyes twinkled despite the bland smile.

Despite her sore bottom, Laura found herself returning a smile. He looked so mischievous standing there. She had a feeling the world didn't see that side of him much.

"It sure is, Mr. Zach," Laura returned, baring her teeth. "I am taking a break, you see...."

"Daddy!" Angela's laughter disappeared. "She fell. I can't make her understand how to hold the horse and mount."

"Perhaps your father can help you, Angela. You two can show me what I'm missing."

Surprise widened the young girl's eyes. Looking at her father, she said nothing.

"Sure, Angela." Zach smiled gratefully at Laura. He climbed over the fence and came toward them. Tall, handsome, and just a hint of beard after being gone for most of the day, he was a bit dusty. Of course, out here where the land was so flat and they had so much wind, she wouldn't expect anything else. She watched his long-legged stride as he crossed the ground. "It's been a while since I helped anyone learn to ride. You were the last one, Angie."

"Dad! I'm Angela. Angie is so-o-o immature."

"You'll always be Angie-doll to me, honey. Now I'll hold the head—"

"I'm teaching her, dad."

Frustration rang in the girl's voice.

"I suppose you are at that," he said softly.

Zach moved over and held out a hand to Laura. "First off, we need to help this pretty lady up," he said.

Angela giggled.

Laura stared at the dark brown hand that reached for her own. Putting her smaller pale one in his, she allowed him to pull her up. Zach caught her, slipping an arm around her.

"And before we let her go..." He turned her hand to examine the burns.

Laura only felt the warmth of the arm around her waist, the comfort of being held close, the safety of having someone there to hold her and share the burden as he examined her hands.

When he looked down at her, though, with attraction in his eyes, Laura felt something more. Laura felt a warmth toward this man bloom.

He stilled his inspection and simply stared at her.

Laura couldn't break his gaze. She stared into the deep brown eyes thinking how wonderful he was as a person, how attractive as a man, and how much she had enjoyed his company the past few days. And how kissable he looked.

"Daddy? Are Miss Laura's hands okay?"

And that he had a daughter standing ten feet away!

Laura blushed.

Zach smiled slightly before releasing her. "I think so. However, we want her to wear gloves while she's doing this. So make sure she slips your gloves on, honey, before she gets on the horse.''

"Can we show her now?"

Zach went over to the head of the horse and held it steady.

Laura watched as Angela demonstrated three different times the correct way to mount a horse. She watched the way the father and daughter worked so well together with the horse and wondered just how many times the two of them had done this together. Their frowns as they concentrated, the way they handled the horse, it was so similar. Did Angela realize she was a tiny replica of her father?

And yet, though she was a replica in many ways, she also had a grace that wasn't present in Zach. Every motion as she mounted the horse and moved a hand cried out *woman*.

Zach probably had heart failure every time he had to deal with a boy coming to his door to date his daughter. And there had to be a lot, Laura thought, watching Angela.

"Your turn," Angela finally said and turned to take control of Jingle Bells.

Zach took the gloves from his daughter and

handed them to Laura. "I can't believe you've never been on a horse," he murmured low as she carefully worked the gloves on her hands.

"What is it about everyone out here?" she muttered. "Even Red made that comment. Not everyone rides horses, you know."

Zach chuckled, the low deep sound sending shivers through her. "Out here, everyone does."

Slipping a hand to her lower back, he led her over to the horse.

"Okay, Miss Laura. Do it like I did." Angela motioned, watching her like a hawk.

Laura looked at the big beast, wondering why she'd decided to do this. She should have found something else Angela liked. Still, she wasn't about to let the mare defeat her.

Putting her hands exactly where Angela had, she worked her left foot into the stirrup.

The horse shifted.

Laura hopped, losing her balance.

Zach chuckled.

"Be still Jingle Bells," Angela admonished.

"Just ignore her dancing, Laura, and boost yourself up."

Laura huffed as she hopped along with the shifting horse. "I'm trying."

Zach covered his mirth poorly. Laura heard it in every word he said. Of course, the muffled snort was a giveaway, too. If she got on the horse, she was going to dance it right over to him, she thought, disgusted.

"All right, all right. I think she needs a little help, Angie-doll."

Laura felt a wide hand shove her up. Her gasp of surprise turned to a gasp of shock as she went up and over and landed with a graceless thud. That didn't stop the grin of pure pride. "I'm sitting on it!"

Zach stepped back and winked at his daughter. "She sure is, isn't she, honey?"

Angela rolled her eyes as would any teenager at a daddy's endearment. Turning importantly to Laura, she put on an air of professionalism. "Now we're going to walk you around the corral. Sit, with your heels down and move with the horse."

Laura did as instructed as Angela guided

the horse by a lead, but her attention was more on the man who walked by her.

Around and around they went, before Angela finally stopped the horse. "Can I go to town now to visit friends, Dad?"

Zach frowned. "You should really finish your chores, Angie."

"Dad!"

Laura saw the disappointment and frustration in the girl's face. Still, that was all she said to her father before sighing. "Yes, sir."

"Thank you so much, Angela, for the riding lesson," Laura said softly.

Angela shrugged. "We can do it again tomorrow if you want."

"I'd like that very much." Laura ached for the girl's disappointment as much as for Zach's sudden frustration. She wondered exactly what was going on here that she didn't see. She was pleased when Angela's eyes brightened at the thought of giving her another lesson. *Well, Father, you were right. She really likes this horse stuff.*

Zach reached up and slipped his hands around Laura's waist, drawing her attention to him. "Now dismount just like you got on."

Laura did, coming to rest on the ground and immediately stumbling.

Zach grabbed her hips, pulling her back against him, holding her tight, steadying her.

"It's from riding the horse," Angela said, giggling. With another muffled laugh, she turned and led Jingle Bells to the stalls.

Laura felt the warmth surround her and sighed, leaning into it briefly. When her legs were steady she nodded. "I wouldn't have dreamed my legs would betray me so. I wasn't on that long."

"Angela walked you almost twenty minutes. You might be a little stiff tomorrow. I have some ointment if you want."

Laura flushed. "I'm in shape. I don't think I'll be hurting that much."

Zach nodded and turned toward the house, cupping her elbow briefly as he made sure she wasn't going to fall flat on her face as they started walking. "I have some paperwork that needs doing."

"Zach..." Laura walked along with him grateful for his consideration while she wondered if she should interfere. Deciding, if she was supposed to be a companion to Angela, she should ask what was on her mind, she geared herself up to confront him.

"Yeah?" He climbed over the fence then turned, helping her over it.

Laura felt the strength as he lowered her to the ground and again was reminded of safety, comfort, caring. "Why do you worry so about Angela leaving the house?"

Zach sighed, his hands going to his hips as he stared off in the distance.

"If I'm to work with your daughter, it'd behoove me to know what's going on here, between the two of you."

"I suppose you're right." He started toward the house, going around toward the back porch. Going up the steps, he held the screen door open then went to a sink and washed up before entering the kitchen.

Laura silently followed, leaving Angela's gloves on a small nearby table. The loud squeak of the screen door to the kitchen reminded her of some old horror movie, and she shuddered.

Inside, Zach poured himself some lemonade before looking to Laura in query. At Laura's nod, he poured her a glass, too.

She seated herself at the old oak table, watching Zach, assessing, trying to determine why such a simple question was so hard to answer.

Zach motioned to the back door. "Company always comes to the back door. Bad news the front door. Ever heard that saying?"

Laura chuckled. "I'm not sure."

Zach allowed a small smile to curve his lips despite the pain in his eyes. "Yeah, you got me there. Well, that's a saying out here. But when it's your brother bringing you the news, bad news can come to the back door, too."

Zach lifted the glass and downed a third of the contents before setting it on the table. "My wife, Carolyn, was a wonderful woman. We fell in love almost immediately. She was supposed to be coming out here to work at the hospital."

A bitter smile twisted his lips. Laura wanted to cry at the look of torment in his eyes.

"But that's not what she was doing," he continued. "She was attached to the hospital with a search-and-rescue team. A team that went out into danger to retrieve the injured. She knew, because of my parents' accident, that I didn't particularly like reckless people or high-risk jobs. To me, life's too important. There's no reason to risk your life just for thrills.''

"How did your parents die?"

"Skydiving. They were always rushing from one thrill to the next, telling me it was the only way to live, to enjoy life to its fullest. They didn't come home from that, and I was left with two brothers to raise and a ranch to hold on to. I was nineteen years old."

Horrified, Laura stared. "Oh, Zach..."

"Anyway. That's not important. What's important is that my wife was following in their footsteps. She got a rush from her job, took stupid risks. I don't know how many times she came home scraped and bruised, even when she was pregnant. Even after the baby was born. And she loved it. The glow in her eyes..."

"There's no sin in liking your job, Zach."

Zach shook his head. "It wasn't that. She drove too fast. If there were extracurricular activities, she had to be the best, had to make it more dangerous for the thrill of it. Don't get me wrong, she loved me and I loved her. But it was history repeating itself.''

Zach ran a hand down his face and sighed. ''Anyway. That's not important. What's important is that my wife took stupid risks. I was twenty-eight, Angie seven, when Mitch, who was apprenticing at the sheriff's office with a deputy, came to the back door. Carolyn had been part of the family for just over eight years before she died.''

Zach ran a hand over his face. ''She was a sister to them. I'll never forget the look on his face. Or how my other brother Julian, Mitch and I sat in the hospital room hour by hour, hoping Carolyn would regain consciousness...but she never did.''

Zach leaned back in his chair, weariness etched in the lines on his face. ''I won't have my daughter following their paths. Bebe, her friend, is wild. And I think Angela is interested in Harry, the kid who's deputy sheriff. He likes to go out and kick up his heels quite a bit. I don't know if he's a Christian, either. If he is, he's not living a productive life.

That's not my call. But when it comes to Angela, keeping her safe, and not letting her follow in my parents' and her mother's footsteps is of utmost importance to me.''

Laura turned the glass, watching the condensation run down and drip onto the scarred tabletop. ''Sometimes we just have to let go and believe that God is in control. Trust Him to guide us and take care of us.''

''God also gave us a brain and gave me the job of taking care of my daughter.''

Smiling slightly, Laura nodded. ''But if she's going to do something, she's going to do it. Just give her love and be there for her, Zach. Don't come down so hard on her that she feels she has to prove something to you. To prove she's adult enough to do whatever it is she wants.''

Zach snorted. ''She's still a kid, she isn't an adult. And I'm not going to let her make the mistakes others have made.''

Okay, so he has a blind spot about this, Laura admitted silently. ''We all make mistakes.''

''And she can make mistakes. She's just not going to risk her life in the process.''

Laura wanted to tell him again to let go of the past and let God have control and then he and Angela could go on. They were both hanging on to the past; he with the memories of the bad, and Angela by trying to be like her mother. That was the only woman she could remember, evidently.

The weight of just what she would represent in the young girl's life felt heavy on her shoulders. *Help me, Father,* she prayed silently. *Help me not to make the situation even worse.*

"Give it to God, Zach. Give Him your broken dreams and let God heal you, let Him guide you in what to do with Angela. I know...I don't remember who I am or what my life was like, but I do know the Bible tells us we have to let go and let God arise."

Zach shook his head. "I have to keep her from getting hurt."

And that was that, Laura thought. There was nothing she could do to help, except pray, and be there for Angela.

And hope that Zach would learn to let go and allow God to handle things instead of trying to fix everything himself. *Teach him, Father. Help him let go and trust You.*

"It'll work out. Now, I should shower before dinner," Zach said and stood.

Laura nodded. "Good idea. Me, too. I feel like I'm more dirt than person at the moment."

"Laura..." Zach started. His gaze swept her, then he shook his head. The look in his eyes faded, and he smiled. "Thank you."

Laura smiled. "Thank you, Zach, for sharing, and not getting angry when I tossed in my two cents' worth."

"Never," he said and turned, heading toward the living room.

Laura watched him leave and felt her heart expand as she did. He was certainly special. Angela was lucky to have a father who loved her so much, as was Zach lucky to have a daughter who loved him in return.

She didn't like that they were at odds. Which only made her determined to get up first thing in the morning and go out and do more bonding with Angela. Be there if she was needed. Because, in her opinion, they both needed a friend right now. Besides,

she'd been through the worst of horse training, falling off that mean horse. She was certain it couldn't be worse. No, indeed. After
today, she was certain it'd be a cinch.

she'd been through the [...]s of bruis[...] and telling herself that no [...] anymore. She [...] in [...] to run. [...]hard[...] and [...]day, she [...]

Chapter Six

It was a cinch, all right. Laura scowled up at the horse, stiff, and nearly unable to move from the pain of riding yesterday. When Angela had suggested working on the horse instead of riding since Laura could only hobble around like an invalid, she'd thought it a grand idea.

"It's not *that* funny," Laura muttered.

Angela's chuckles drifted off and she covered her grin with her hand before she went over, giving Laura a hand up. She giggled when Laura groaned every inch of the way up. "I told you to be careful. Jingle Bells likes to puff out her sides."

"The cinch was tight."

Angela shook her head and moved over to replace the saddle. "Now watch this." Angela lifted a knee and pushed it into Jingle Bells.

Jingle Bells' side deflated.

Angela immediately tightened the strap a second time.

"All horses do that. Well, most of them anyway. I will admit, she usually doesn't do it with me. Maybe because you're a new rider she thought she could get away with it."

Laura glared at the horse.

The horse smiled at her.

"Yeah. Maybe that's it."

The horse snorted shaking its head at Laura then turned its attention away.

"It hates me."

"Don't be silly," Angela said. "Jingle Bells doesn't hate you. And Jingle Bells is a *she* not *it*."

"I stand corrected." Laura stretched, trying to remember again why she had agreed to come out here and get on the demon horse.

"You're not doing too bad, Miss Laura. Really. It just takes time to learn."

Angela went over and stroked the dark skin of the horse. "This horse is a really good animal. She had some of the best parents, durable, sturdy. We really didn't think she was going to live when she was born."

Angela stroked her neck again, smiling softly. "But she did. Daddy says I should pick one of the other horses to ride regularly, but Jingle Bells and I have been together too long."

Laura pushed herself up and dusted off her clothes. "Really?"

Angela nodded. "I think I told you a bit about the story earlier. This horse was born from the horse my mom used to ride."

"You miss your mom?" Laura walked over and stood next to Angela, trying not to feel as if the horse were smirking at her.

"I don't really remember her. Besides, she didn't like the ranch and I do."

Laura's heart went out to the young girl as, for some reason, that sounded like such a lonely statement. "I wish I could remember who I was."

Angela glanced over curiously at Laura. "What's it like, not to remember anything?"

Reaching out, she checked the cinch like Angela had shown her, muttering when the horse danced away. "It's, like…umph…there is nothing there except…frustration. Yeah, frustration, pain and fear. I wonder why I can't remember. If the pain and injury caused the memory loss, or was it the fear as the car rolled? Why can't I remember? I'll be talking and say some things fine, and yet the next sentence I can't even remember if I've ever been on a ranch when someone asks, and the shock of being reminded I can't remember is quite unsettling."

"Why did God let it happen? Why does He let bad things happen? Have you ever wondered that?"

Laura backed away from the horse. "You know, I think God is God. Things happen. He can see the entire picture of what's going on, which direction our life is headed, what's ahead for us. I think he's perfecting us, refining us for a time when we'll be with Him."

"Like my mom," Angela whispered.

"I pray sometimes that if there is a reason I'm not going to make it to the finish line, that I'm going to fall away, that God takes me before that happens or does what is necessary to get me back on track and in His will. Sometimes our experiences are painful—after all, I don't like having no memory—but it's worth it in the end."

"You said you pray sometimes!" Angela's excitement cut through Laura's words.

"How about that? See what I mean about my Swiss cheese brain?" Chuckling, she moved to Angela's other side. "Some things I remember, others…"

Dusting off the arms of her long-sleeved shirt, she said, "So, let's get on with this teaching me how to saddle this wonderful animal. Then I can get on and you can teach me again how to walk around the yard." Laura thought, *So I can get up in the morning and not be able to move again.* Still, it was worth it since Angela seemed to have opened up and started talking to her.

"Great!" Angela gave one last pat and then set about instructing Laura in the proper way to saddle and sit a horse.

"She gets along great with Angela."

Zach glanced over at his brother who stood

with him near the office window, gazing out at the woman and the girl as they worked on saddling Jingle Bells. "Yeah, she does."

Mitch let the curtain drop and strode over to the sofa, dropping down on it and stretching out his legs. "She still has no idea who she is?"

Zach reluctantly left the window and went over to the desk to lean against it. "Not a clue. Occasionally, when she's talking, something she remembers will just pop out, but she can't connect why she recalls some things and not others."

"How are her hands doing?"

Zach rubbed at his neck. "She hasn't said anything about them, but they're scarred up pretty bad. I'm afraid any fingerprints you get aren't going to help much."

Mitch shook his head. "Feels like God is against us in this one."

Zach's gaze jerked to Mitch's. "You know better than that, Mitch. God is in control."

Mitch shrugged. "Sometimes in my job, you have to wonder. Anyway, I'd like to find out who this woman is and then maybe that would help her get her memory back."

"Yeah." Zach walked back over to the window and pushed the sheer curtain aside again and stared out across the yard toward the stables. "I think she's having nightmares, Mitch. I've heard her moving around at odd hours and the next morning she gets up and looks like she hasn't slept a wink. Whatever is bothering her...I'm wondering if that could be keeping her from remembering. Or maybe it's just that wreck."

"I remember the nightmares Julian and I had when Mom and Dad died. We blocked out months of things to avoid having to face their deaths."

"If we could get some more information on her, the nightmares might subside."

Zach watched as the woman called Laura awkwardly remounted Jingle Bells while his daughter held the head of the horse. Laura was beautiful. The way her hair swung around her as she seated herself, the grin she shot at his daughter. Why had he never really noticed just how beautiful she was before? Maybe because he'd been so caught up in doing the right thing he'd had no time to notice anything else.

"Hey, big brother."

Zach realized Mitch had been talking to him. Turning, he flushed at Mitch's knowing look. "Anyway, if you want to give her a few more days to adjust, for her hands to finish healing..."

Mitch nodded. "There's no hurry. I've sent out feelers to see if anyone has reported a missing person who matches her description. Nothing back yet. No one in town seems to know the woman, either. So, I imagine you were right. She was coming here about the job."

Zach glanced back out the window before turning and heading toward the door. "Looks like she's doing fine. Why don't you come on out and talk to her? I'm sure Angela would like to see you, too."

Mitch stood and walked up by Zach. Zach couldn't miss his smile and knew it was because of the way he'd been staring at Laura. He wasn't sure why he'd been doing it himself, so he wasn't about to discuss it with his younger brother. "She is adjusting to being here. She wants to help, but her hands... I'm not really happy with her working on the horses, but at least she isn't doing too much and is wearing protective gloves.''

"If she wants to help, letting her might be beneficial. It might help trigger her memories.''

"Perhaps,'' Zach acknowledged.

"Uncle Mitch!'' Angela turned from the horse and shot across the corral to where he and Mitch approached the fence.

Mitch grinned then shouted, "Watch out!''

Zach saw the problem and vaulted over the fence, heading toward Jingle Bells, just in time to catch Laura as she went sliding off, right over the top of the horse's head.

Her soft body slammed against his. He closed his arms around her, stumbling back, trying to keep them both from hitting the ground.

It didn't work, and he went down with a thud, Laura right on top of him.

Jarred, Zach lay there, waiting for his breath to return. And as he did, he realized how good it felt to have protected this woman from injury, to hold her close, just to feel the companionship of having someone close.

"It did it again. That horse hates me.''

Zach heard the words she mumbled into his chest and couldn't resist a chuckle. "I doubt that, Laura." Zach saw Mitch and Angela standing over them and nodded to Mitch for help.

Mitch moved forward, and Zach met Laura's eyes as Mitch helped her up. He saw something in them—thanks, perhaps, or maybe it was an acknowledgment of feelings, too. He wasn't sure.

"I'm so sorry, Miss Laura. I didn't think."

Laura turned to Angela and smiled, a beautiful smile of understanding. "It's perfectly all right. We all make mistakes occasionally. Besides, your dad there saved me."

Zach stood, dusting himself off. He was surprised when Angela turned, grinning. "You sure did, Dad. I didn't know you could move that fast."

Mitch laughed.

Zach looked outraged. "For an old man, you mean?"

Angela giggled. "Ancient."

Zach growled at his daughter and feinted, before jumping forward and grabbing her around the waist. "I'll show you old."

"Daddy! Daddy!"

Zach reveled as he swung her around in the air before dropping her to the ground. "Now, take care of that horse. Uncle Mitch has to talk to Laura."

"I'm an adult, Daddy. You are not supposed to swing an adult around."

Zach grinned at his flushing daughter as she shoved her hair behind her ear and turned. He watched her scamper off to the horse, looking part adult, part kid.

"She's something else," Mitch observed, chuckling.

"Yeah, she is." Turning back to Laura, he said, "I hope you don't mind answering some questions."

"Not at all." Laura's soft smile left and a purely professional aura surrounded her. "Now, how can I help you Mitch?" Mitch took Laura's elbow and escorted her back toward the house as he talked. "Well, ma'am, we haven't been able to find anyone searching for you. I'd like to ask you some questions, see if anything might be triggered. And also, ask you if you feel up to fingerprints yet."

Zach followed quietly, wondering when his brother had grown up. It seemed like only yesterday Mitch was the wild one, the boy without direction. And here he was handling this case so professionally. Pride touched his heart.

Opening the door, he waited for them to enter then followed them into the living room.

Laura pulled off the gloves as she seated herself on the overstuffed sofa, relaxing into it. She held her hands out to Mitch for examination.

Zach looked at the scarred, rough places on her hands and especially her fingers. His heart went out to her as he looked at them.

Laura flipped her hands over. "I'm not sure you'll get too many good prints. One, maybe two fingers here might be undamaged enough for that."

"You know about fingerprints?" Mitch asked, surprised.

Laura looked surprised, too. "I—I don't know. Maybe I've read about them. I know I like to read. Or maybe I have a job...."

Zach watched her brow furrow as she tried to remember. When her hand went to her forehead he moved over next to her and touched her hand. The bright red looked so tender as he cupped it between his own two hands. "It's okay, Laura. It'll come to you soon. Just give it time."

Her fingers curled around his hand, and Zach was certain she derived comfort from his touch. Lifting his gaze to hers, he saw her bright-blue eyes staring with wide-eyed surprise into his. Surprise and...attraction.

So, she was attracted to him too, was she? Why he felt so relieved to know that, he wasn't sure. She was his responsibility. And she had no memory. He shouldn't be feeling this way about her.

"Ahem."

Zach glanced at Mitch. "Go on with your questioning," he said, though he didn't release her hand. "Just take it easy."

Mitch's mouth quirked. Turning back to Laura, he began. "That night, do you remember anything at all?"

Laura shook her head. "No. I...I don't."

"What's the last thing you remember?"

Her hand tightened in Zach's. He doubted she even realized it as she had her full concentration on Mitch. "I— Darkness. I remember darkness and then the sound of beeping. Eventually there was a fog. And then someone in white—a nurse. Then Zach."

Zach gently squeezed her hand reassuring her that all was fine.

Mitch wrote in his notebook. "You've had some flashbacks, it seems. Things you've remembered since then."

"No, not really. I..." Laura hesitated. "They seem just to pop out when I'm talking. Nothing I remember exactly. I do know abstract things, for instance. I like the circus and enjoy caramel apples. But if you ask me when I've ever been to the circus or eaten apples, I can't tell you that. It's very frustrating, knowing things but not having the memories to back them up."

Mitch nodded before reaching out and patting her arm. "That's fine, Miss Laura. Now, tell me, have you been having nightmares?"

Her hand tightened spasmodically on Zach's before going limp. "No. Not at all. I'm not sure why you'd think I would."

Zach frowned, looking in confusion at Mitch. He knew she was lying. He'd heard her up and around…her reaction proved it, he would say.

"I see. Have you been sleeping through the night then?" Mitch pursued.

Laura shook her head. "Actually, no. I sleep a few hours and then wake up. I imagine I'm just restless or I'm not used to a lot of sleep. I'm not sure the reason. At any rate, twice now I've awoken with trouble getting back to sleep. That's one reason I want to do some work around the house." Laura shot a look at Zach before turning back to Mitch. "I'm restless and want something to fill my time."

Mitch grinned. "Well, I don't see a problem with that. The work should do you good."

Zach groaned. "Thanks, little brother."

Smiling superiorly, Laura said to Zach, "See, even your brother agrees with me. Thanks, Mitch. Maybe you can get this hard-headed protector to listen to me."

Mitch grinned. "Very observant. Most people think Zach is simply grumpy and unreasonable, not realizing he's simply a protector."

Zach scowled. "Okay, you two. Stop dissecting me here in front of me."

"You never did like that, did you, Zach?" Mitch said, grinning.

"I'm big enough to show you how much I don't like it, too," he said, still scowling though there was no heat behind his words. He knew Mitch was simply trying to put Laura at ease. And he thanked God he had a relationship with his brothers that he could joke with them. Sometimes that was the only thing that got them through the hard times.

"I'll take you up on that at the local town party in a few weeks. As it is—" Mitch turned his attention back to Laura and smiled gently "—I'll look into this further. Call me if you need or remember anything."

"Thank you, Mitch."

Mitch stood and headed toward the door. Laura and Zach walked with him to the door.

"You have a good brother," Laura said, watching Mitch leave. "And a good daughter."

Zach smiled. "Yeah, I do. And an intelligent one, too. So, Laura, how would you officially like the job as housekeeper here, to help my daughter out? It seems you're ready to work and my daughter likes you. I couldn't ask for anything more. Think you can handle it?''

Laura grinned. "I sure can. I've been bored stiff with nothing to do."

"You be careful with those hands and the job is yours."

Laura nodded, her smile lighting up the room. "No problem. After all, housekeeping is easy and it'll keep me occupied. Keeping my hands out of trouble will be no problem."

Chapter Seven

❧

"Did I say housekeeping was easy? Did I? I had to be crazy! No, it's your fault. All your fault. You had a mind of your own. You are the one who thought making caramel popcorn balls would be cool."

Laura stared at her hands in disgust. "No, my brain took a vacation so it has to be your fault," she said to her hands, still muttering, picking at the caramel that seemed glued to her hands. "Ugh. What a mess."

"Who're you talking to?"

Laura jumped and whirled. "Zach! Umm...no one. What are you doing back to the house so early? Angela won't be back for an hour and I thought well—''

"What are you making?"

Glancing down, she saw popcorn covered with caramel. "Popcorn balls. Or, it was suppose to be."

"Ah, I see. You forgot the butter."

"Butter?"

"For your hands."

Laura looked down at her hands in dismay. "That's why the caramel is sticking."

Zach chuckled and lifted the pan of caramel corn and set it aside. "Let a pro show you how to do this." Slipping a hand to her back, he escorted her over to the sink and filled it with warm soapy water. "Wash that off, then pop some more popcorn. I'll get some more caramel down. So, how did you figure out we liked caramel corn?"

Laura slipped her hands into the warm water and gently, carefully, scrubbed all the caramel off her hands. "Well, it could be the fact you had six bags of unpopped popcorn up there and ten caramel mixes."

"Hey, the only time our local store carries

the caramel is in October. I have to stock up.''

Laura glanced sideways at him, grinning. "Of course."

The light in his eyes, the way his features relaxed, made him look almost boyish. "Yep."

Drying off her hands, she watched as he expertly started melting the gooey mixture. "You know your way around the kitchen."

"I raised my two brothers and then Angela when Carolyn died. Someone had to cook. My brothers and I took turns."

"Where are your brothers now?" Laura pulled out the popcorn and measured out a fresh batch into the popper.

"Well, Mitch, you know. He's the sheriff. He moved out when Carolyn and I were having problems. Besides, as sheriff it was better for him to be closer to town. Julian is studying to be a doctor. He's here in the summers, but in school the rest of the time. He's just finishing up his studies and should be choosing somewhere to go soon."

Laura watched the popcorn as it popped. "He's not coming back here?"

Zach shrugged. "I imagine he'll follow his heart. He isn't too enthusiastic about staying here. With two big brothers, he feels like he's under constant scrutiny. We'll see. I'm praying he follows God's direction. Although, we could sure use a new doctor around here."

"Here we go." She dumped the popcorn into another large pan.

"Perfect." Zach continued to stir the caramel before turning the fire down low. "Get out the butter now and bring it over here."

Laura followed his orders, setting it next to him. She was surprised when he paused in his stirring and turned to her. "Hold out your hands."

He grabbed a cooking spoon and scooped out some butter and plopped it in her hands.

"Oh yuck. What am I supposed to do with this?"

Zach grinned. "You mean I have to show you?" A devilish light entered his eyes, and he reached out.

"Uh, Zach..."

She didn't like that look one bit. But she couldn't break his gaze. His eyes were so full of life, of energy. She vaguely realized he was reaching for her hand. But that was far from her mind as she was caught up in the simple emotions shining on his features.

At least, she was until she felt his hand close around hers and butter squished everywhere. "Zach!"

His rich chuckle ran over her. "Now, Laurie-pie, dontcha know that's what we have to do. It has to be all over your hands so the caramel won't stick."

She watched him, his strong dark hands as they smoothed a thin layer of butter all over her hands before slicking his own.

Grabbing up the pan he proceeded to pour the golden mixture over the popped corn. "Now it'll work. Come on." Laura moved up next to him and tentatively stuck her hands into the dish and smiled when her hands didn't come away with goo on them. "It didn't say this on the directions," she muttered.

He chuckled, his shoulder brushing hers as he worked the mixture together and started forming balls. "Why did you want to make these, anyway?"

"I know there's a town party coming up

and thought we could take these. And besides, I thought Angela might like them. She said something about them the other day when we were working on saddling the horse.''

Zach frowned. ''Yeah. She does. It's been a while since we fixed any, though.''

''It's no big deal. Sometimes life gets in the way, Zach and we forget to take time for the fun things.'' It was Laura's turn to frown as those words rang in her head.

''Laura, hon, what is it?''

She resumed her task of making caramel balls, shaking the odd feeling away. ''I don't know. Those words—they just seemed familiar somehow. But I can't...''

Laura paused again, trying to pull the image that accompanied those words into focus. ''Ow...'' Shaking her head, she lifted a wrist to press on her forehead. ''It hurts to try to remember.''

A strong warm hand closed over hers, pulling it away from her head. ''Give it time, Laura. You'll remember.''

Gentle caring and concern radiated from him. Laura wanted to sink into that comfort, revel in it, enjoy it...his warm hands around hers, the tender way he held her hands, his thumb stroking the top of her hand.

"You have caramel on your forehead."

Her eyes widened. "What?"

The corners of his mouth turned up. "Caramel. On your forehead."

Laura groaned, going pink. "I'm a total mess, aren't I?"

Zach slowly shook his head. "I think you look lovely."

When he leaned forward, Laura couldn't believe it. Surely he wasn't going to... Not here. She... Oh my...

Her eyes drifted closed as his lips touched her forehead. Warmth, security and desire ran through her. Tears touched her eyes. Yes, she wanted this. *Oh, Father, this is so right. I feel like I've been alone forever.*

"Daddy?"

The slamming of the back door jerked them apart. Laura stared at him stunned, realizing suddenly what she had been thinking and what had just happened.

The look in his own eyes was just as stunned. He quickly covered it as Angela came bounding into the kitchen. She looked from Laura to her father, then at the popcorn balls. "All right! You made me popcorn balls, Dad!"

Zach chuckled, though to Laura's ears it sounded a bit strained. "Well actually, Laura started them and I just finished them with her."

"Can I help?" Angela came over and looked into the pan.

"Sure."

Laura forced a smile. "That'd be great. I don't know why I didn't ask you originally. Just don't forget to put butter on your hands."

Angela rolled her eyes. "Who would forget something like that?"

Laura met Zach's eyes over her head, and he chuckled before turning his attention back to the task at hand. However, he didn't break her gaze quickly enough for Laura to miss the disconcerting look in his eyes.

Laura moved next to Angela and started working with her as she reminded herself she had no memory, didn't know anything about her past, and had no business being attracted to this man, any man for that matter. Besides, she was only there temporarily as a house-keeper. She didn't know what would happen from one day to the next.

No, attraction was not a good thing at all.

However, Laura realized dismally, one couldn't control emotions and feelings.

Guide me, Father. I don't know why I'm feeling this. I don't want to feel this. Help me, direct me, in my life. But most importantly, please, God, please help me get my memory back before I do something really stupid.

"Well, as much fun as this has been, I did only come to the house for some paperwork. I'm headed into town." Going over to the the sink, he washed his hands. "As for you..." he said coming over to Angela. After only a slight hesitation, he leaned down and kissed her on her head.

"Daddy!"

Laura met his gaze and nodded.

Zach glanced back down at his daughter and kissed her again, then chuckled. "You be good and help Miss Laura out while I'm gone. We don't want her getting bored and wandering off."

Angela, like a typical teenager, rolled her eyes again. To Laura, he said, "My cell phone number is on the desk or you can ask Angela. If you need me, call. You, too, squirt," he added to Angela and headed into the other room, ignoring Angela's squawk of displeasure.

"Why does he call me names like that?" Angela muttered.

Laura finished up her last popcorn ball and grinned. "Because he loves you. I wish I had someone to call me nicknames."

"You don't remember anything?" Angela asked, suddenly awkward and uncomfortable.

"I sure don't, honey." A dark cloud descended but she mentally pushed it away. "However, if I do, you'll be the first one to know. How's that?"

"Really?" Angela brightened considerably.

"Yeah."

"Way cool." The popcorn balls finished, Angela moved to the water to wash her hands. "Hey, I have a nickname! Can I call you Laurie?"

Laura's hands stilled as the name floated

through her, raising the hairs on the back of her neck.

"I mean, if you don't want me to—"

"No. No. I like that."

"Are we still going on the picnic?" Angela casually asked.

"Oh!" Shocked, Laura realized she'd forgotten. A few days ago, Angela had asked about going to her favorite spot. Laura had suggested turning it into a picnic. "I can't believe I nearly forgot that. Yes. We are. You get whatever we'll need and I'll pack the food. How's that?"

Angela nodded. Just as she got to the door, she paused. "Do you like my dad?"

"Uh, well…" Laura swallowed and then swallowed again. "Yeah. Your dad seems like a nice guy. Who else would take someone in they didn't even know?"

Angela turned and studied Laura with a look that wasn't very teenagerish at all before she finally she nodded. "I guess he's okay."

Resuming her teenager demeanor, she bounded out of the kitchen and across the compound.

"Okay? Well, I suppose that's better than nothing."

"Zach!" Laura whirled, clutching her chest. "Boots are supposed to make noise. You scared ten years off me."

Zach chuckled. "I just wanted to let you know I was leaving."

Laura nodded. As her surprise and shock left, worry and embarrassment replaced it. Had he heard everything she had said? "We're going on a picnic. I'm going to pack the food while Angela gets the horses ready."

"Ah." Zach nodded gravely. "And where is Angela taking you on the picnic?"

"She said down by a creek with a good tree to swing on, whatever that means. I think she likes the spot, though."

A corner of Zach's mouth quirked up revealing a dimple. "Yeah. I know the spot. Mitch used to take her there a lot. It was his favorite spot, too."

Laura heard the yearning in Zach's voice and wondered. "Did you ever go with her?"

Zach shrugged. "When I could. My brothers were still young. I was trying to save the ranch. I lost a lot of years with Angie, Laura.

It's not something I'm proud of, but I was in a struggle to save the ranch, keep a roof over our heads, not just for me, Carolyn and Angie, but Mitch and Julian, too.''

"It sounds like something that I can't even imagine. I'm sure they understand.''

"Angie doesn't.''

"Give her time.''

Zach's features were inscrutable, neither agreeing nor disagreeing with her plea. "Are you up to riding a horse?'' he finally asked.

Laura looked at her hands. "They're getting better. I think, with gloves, they'll be okay. The spots on my side and arm are peeling.'' She wrinkled her nose. "The only problem I might have is that insane horse from—''

Zach burst out in chuckles. "Excuse me?''

"You don't have to sound so incredulous. You heard me right.''

Laura knew she sounded like she was pouting, but no one would believe her about that mad horse. She knew she wasn't imagining that Jingle Bells was out to get her. She had the bruised toes, and posterior, to prove it.

"Jingle Bells is very mild mannered. Angela has trained her nearly from birth. She loves the horse. Jingle Bells has never harmed a hair on her head.''

''She's still got it in for me,'' Laura refuted stubbornly.

Zach shook his head, grinning. ''If you say so.''

''It doesn't matter if I say so or not, you just watch her next time I'm around her. Something will happen. It always does.''

''We could try a different horse. But I'm afraid your skills just aren't up to it. Jingle Bells is the oldest and easiest to work with.''

''Then please, don't even think about changing horses on me. I'd end up trampled.''

''You know, Laura, I would just bet the horse senses your fear and is reacting to that. Perhaps that's why you keep having problems. Don't let her sense your fear and everything should be fine.''

Laura thought about it—hard. Had she been projecting fear every time she got near the horse? Perhaps. Just perhaps, she had. ''Okay. I'll try it.''

Going over to the refrigerator she pulled it

open. "And I'd better get on lunch or Angela is going to wonder what is keeping me."

"Have fun."

There was a hesitation and then he headed toward the door. "If you get home early," Laura said quickly, though not turning when she did, "you can come on out and join us if you want."

Zach paused. Silence descend Laura's hands stilled on the lettuce.

Finally, he spoke. "I just might do that."

Relief eased the tension in her, and she smiled at the tomato she was holding. "Great."

"Oh, and Laura?"

Hands full, she backed out of the fridge. "Yes?"

"I think you're pretty nice, too."

Laura gasped, losing hold of the items in her hands. As the food tumbled, she swore to herself she hadn't heard what she thought she had. She whirled to confront Zach, but the only thing she saw was the swinging of the kitchen door that announced her tormentor had just made clean his escape after dropping that bombshell.

Bending down, she started gathering the veggies she'd dropped. "And I thought the horse liked to provoke. Zach McCade, I swear you're as bad as that demented animal."

Still, inside though, she glowed from Zach's words.

Chapter Eight

❧

"It wasn't that bad, Miss Laura."

Laura worked to relax on the animal she rode. "I ended up face first on the saddle instead of the saddle ending up on the horse. I don't think I'm ever going to learn how to put a saddle on this horse without some major disaster happening."

Giggling, Angela replied, "She only stepped aside as you swung it around."

Laura scowled between Jingle Bells' ears. "You're listening to this and enjoying every minute."

Show no fear. Well, she hadn't. She'd gone out, stood right in front of the horse and told her she didn't fear her and what was she going to do about that?

She'd found out. The mangy creature side-stepped quicker than she realized the horse could move, and when she tried to compensate she'd lost her balance and had fallen.

Looking around now at the flat plains and tall prairie grass dotted along the trail with mesquite trees, Laura thought of how her life had taken such a turn. "You know, I have to wonder if this is familiar to me or not. It is certainly beautiful in its own way."

"I suppose. I'd like to go where everything is green, though. Where it rains a lot. Where friends are next door instead of an hour's drive. That'd be cool."

Laura grinned. "Cool, huh? I don't know. It's pretty peaceful out here, and you have neighbors nearby. And the church you have is a nice size. Small, but the people love God."

Angela grimaced. "But we hardly ever see them. The town celebration isn't until next week, and I have to wait that long to see—" Angela broke off, shooting a guilty look at Laura.

"The boy you like?"

Angela hesitated and then nodded. "Look, over there. That's where we're going. I'll race you."

Laura groaned as Angela took off, and Jingle Bells decided to take off after her. "Ouch!" *Bang!*—her bottom slapped down hard against the saddle. "You stupid... ouch—" *bam* "—horse. Slow...ouch!" *Slap.* "An-ge-laaa—oh-oh, no, don't you...ouch... dare!"

Laura saw the trees, the river growing larger as the horse raced along toward it. She held on tight, jerking on the reins, kicking at the horse, trying to halt the horse.

Angela pulled to a halt and got off her horse and turned. Laura saw that as Jingle Bells headed right to the creek and stopped, lowering his head.

Laura went tumbling, head over heels. Fear shot through her, just before water closed over her head and she impacted hard against the creek bed.

"Are you okay?"

Struggling up, Laura shoved at her hair. "I—I—I'm fine, just wet." Getting to her knees she gathered up her hair and twisted it to get the excess water out.

The horse nudged her and she fell forward.

"Jingle Bells!"

Laura heard the shout as she came back up out of the water. Reeling to her feet, she swung around to glare at the horse.

Angela had hold of it. "I have no idea why she did that. Maybe she thought she was trying to help you out of the water."

"I told you, the horse doesn't like me." Laura watched the horse eye her.

Angela, of course, missed it since she was in the process of hobbling the horse. "It's okay. You'll learn, and the horse will calm down when you have more control. Maybe I shouldn't have had you ride out this far so soon."

At Angela's fretting, Laura reassured her. "I was asking questions that made you uncomfortable, Angela. Don't worry about it."

Angela, looking unsure, replied, "They don't make me uncomfortable, exactly. Daddy just doesn't understand. He thinks all boys aren't good enough for me. He's very overprotective."

Laura made her way out of the water to the shore. "I imagine he worries."

Angela pulled down the picnic basket and her rifle, propping the weapon against a nearby tree and then opening up the basket to pull out a thin sheet that she tossed out on the ground. "Daddy thinks I'm going to turn out like my mom."

Laura pulled off her tennis shoes and dropped them on a nearby rock, hoping the bright sunshine would dry them and her out. "Oh?"

"He doesn't want me to be wild and a risk-taker like her."

"You don't remember much about your mom?"

Angela shrugged and sprawled out on the sheet. "It doesn't matter. I have Daddy and Uncle Mitch and Uncle Julian."

"So, tell me about this boy."

Angela cut her gaze to Laura.

Laura grinned. "I can't remember anything. Might as well fill my mind with all kinds of other things."

Rolling her eyes, Angela groaned. "Okay. But don't tell Daddy. I think Harry likes me.

He's only nineteen. Wants to be the next sheriff when Uncle Mitch gets tired of it one day. He comes out all the time and always makes a point of talking to me. Seems like a real nice guy.''

Angela frowned. "He does have a bit of temper, but then, so does Daddy."

Laura grinned. "Sounds like a wonderful guy."

Shrugging, Angela said, "He asked me if I'd dance with him at the party. I hadn't planned on going. But, well, maybe I can get a dress and go ahead and go. Miss Laura, I don't own too many dresses. I wear pants to church a lot and then I do have a couple of suits for choral in school if we go sing. That's about it."

"I see." Laura looked down in disgust. "Doesn't look like I'm going to dry anytime soon." Moving over, she plopped down on the sheet near Angela and started setting out food. "Why don't we go shopping tomorrow and just see what they have?"

Laura said this matter-of-factly as she finished setting everything out. She was surprised when Angela responded the way she did.

"Really? That'd be cool! I'd love to get away from the ranch for a while."

All kid, Laura thought, smiling at Angela. Wanting so badly to try her wings. "I'll talk to your dad and see if he minds us going. How's that?"

Angela fixed two plates and handed one to Laura and then sat back to eat her own sandwich. "Better than me asking. All he wants me to do is stay on this ranch."

"Well, we'll see what he says. I really think your father has your best interests at heart."

Angela sighed and looked completely miserable. "I guess he does. But why can't he trust me?"

Laura took a bite of her bread and chewed thoughtfully. "Maybe he doesn't trust others, or he just hasn't seen you as an adult yet. I would imagine it's hard to see someone who you've raised turn into an adult. Some people might not recognize it, or accept it."

"You sound like you speak from experience."

Laura sighed. "I wish I knew. So far, all I know is I burned my hands and knew enough about the burns to know your uncle probably wouldn't get good fingerprints."

Angela looked down at Laura's hands. "Do they hurt much?"

Setting her plate down, Laura smiled. "A bit." She held out one pink-and-white hand. "They look awful, but thankfully not all of the burns were that bad. I should keep most of the use of both my hands. My right thumb, though..." She held up the digit. "It's very stiff. It's going to take a lot of work."

She flipped her hands over. "These are healing. You should see the huge bruise higher on my arm. The thing is black. I wonder how long it's going to take for the bruise to leave?"

Sighing she picked up her food and continued to eat. "But I'm lucky. My car was burned beyond recognition. They say the gas tank must have gone up in flames. God watches over us, doesn't He?"

She winked at Angela, then offered her a hand when the girl kept looking at it. Tentatively Angela reached out and after a hesitation, ran a finger over Laura's hand. "It feels almost like plastic."

"Mmm-hmm. As the skin heals the doctor said not all of it would remain this way. But I will have scars."

"Will it bother you to have scars?"

"No. I don't think so. God saved my life, what's a few scars. Angela, have you ever considered going into the medical field?"

Angela looked up and frowned. "Daddy wouldn't like that. Mama did that. That's what got her killed." Finishing the last of her drink, Angela stood. "I have to go to the bathroom. And well, out here—" Angela motioned toward the brush lining the creek bed in both directions "—that is the um, well, you know."

Laura chuckled. "Yeah, I know. Go on. I'm not going anywhere."

Laura finished her sandwich and tea and then started repacking everything. "The medical field can be relatively safe. If you ease the subject on your dad, he might just eventually be receptive to it when he realizes that's what you want, if you want it."

Angela called out from the bushes, "Yeah, well, pigs fly, too."

"Now you sound like your father, Angela." Laura laughed outright. She picked up the picnic basket and walked over to the tree to deposit the burden just as Angela came back toward her.

Had she not been right there, Laura didn't know what her reaction would have been when Angela suddenly stumbled, fell...and she spotted the rattler right in front of Angela on a nearby rock.

She'd probably never know. Still, as the rattler lifted its tail and rattled out its warning and Angela's eyes widened, Laura didn't think twice as she dropped the basket, jerked up the rifle and shot.

The noise ended abruptly as the head was cleanly severed from the body. But suddenly it wasn't the snake she was seeing but a black picture with bullet holes in it. Noise surrounded her. Noise and laughter and her hands itched with a need to... And it was gone. What had she just seen? Felt?

"Oh...oh!" Angela cried out, jerking

Laura's attention from the remnants of a memory and back to the situation at hand.

Laura dropped the gun and ran the few feet to Angela, who was scrubbing at her face. "Oh, Laura, it got...stuff on me. I know it did!"

"Shush now," Laura said, pulling Angela into her arms.

The girl broke down and started crying, clutching at Laura.

"We'll get anything off. The snake's dead. You're going to be fine." And I'm going to throw up, she silently thought as her whole body shook at the thought of that snake getting Angela.

"You didn't tell me you could use a rifle, Miss Laura. I just knew..."

The girl shuddered and hugged Laura tighter.

"Well, how about that, Angela, you just discovered another one of the secrets in my Swiss cheese brain. I can use a rifle."

That cured Angela's fear as she leaned back, wide-eyed. "I did? Oh, cool. It almost killed me. I wasn't watching and it would have struck if you hadn't shot it. Daddy's not going to believe it when I tell him you saved my life.''

''Oh, no, wait, Angie. I didn't save your life.''

Eyes glowing, Angela nodded. ''Yeah, you did, Miss Laura—Laurie.'' Grinning she nodded again.

Trying to get her mind off it, Laura waved at the tree. ''Why don't you show me now, why this tree is so important and just where you swing off it. Maybe we can bask a few hours here in the sun while my clothes dry and talk about shopping tomorrow.''

Angela's mind turned from the subject of the snake and she nodded. ''Sure. And, Thank you, L-Laurie for saving me.''

Oh, well, so maybe it hadn't. Standing, Laura helped Angela stand and together they finished putting everything up before they both went to the tree where Angela could show Laura just how to swing from the branches.

And the entire time, Laura feared that Angela's opinion on how Zach was going to react wasn't right at all. She was afraid it might have just the opposite effect. Unless she confided about the wisp of memory she'd seen. But did she want to tell him that with his attitude toward everything she'd heard so far? She'd find out soon enough.

Chapter Nine

"You should have seen her, Daddy. I just knew I'd really done something clumsy and then the head went flying off faster than I could imagine."

Angela shuddered and took another bite of baked beans before picking up her hamburger.

Embarrassed, Laura glanced down at her own plate. "It was... I'm not sure, instinct maybe."

"Thank you, for saving her life, Laura. And Angela, we'll have a talk about being a bit more careful later."

Angela grinned. "You don't have to tell

me to be careful. Not after that. May I be excused?''

Zach nodded.

Angela jumped up, grabbing her plate and some of the other empty dishes she went into the kitchen.

When she was gone, Laura finally met Zach's gaze.

''She could have died.''

Reacting to the unsteadiness she heard in Zach's voice, Laura laid down her fork and reached across the table to squeeze his hand. ''God was watching over her.''

''I do my best to protect her. Sometimes just...''

Laura squeezed his hand again. ''Try to eat something. That might help some.''

Zach squeezed her hand tightly. ''No. I— So you know how to shoot a gun.''

''Evidently.''

''A good idea for anyone on a ranch. I wonder where you learned it.''

Laura didn't say anything until he lifted his gaze to hers. ''I remembered something. A gun, in my hands, and a target. Noisy, laughing. Somewhere inside a building.''

"A shooting range." Zach nodded. "I'm not surprised. If you shoot as well as Angie said, then you learned on a ranch or in a range somewhere. That's not something you 'just do.'"

"No, it's not."

Zach leaned back in his chair, only then releasing Laura's hand. Laura felt the loss of contact but didn't comment. The way Zach glanced at their hands briefly told her he'd probably forgotten he was even holding it. "My wife—Carolyn—couldn't shoot. She could do everything else, though. Rappelling, mountain climbing. You name it, she did it. She thought she could shoot, but she couldn't hit the side of a barn. Of course, that was Carolyn. Everything she did she did with all of her being, believing she could do it whether she could or couldn't."

Zach grinned, the heaviness temporarily lifting. "She loved people and would do anything for them, too. I fell hopelessly in love."

Laura nodded and pushed her own plate away before crossing her arms on the yellow linen tablecloth.

"It almost killed me when she died. And

now I see Angie trying to follow in her footsteps.''

Angela came walking back out and Zach broke off. ''Finish loading the dishes and then the rest of the night is yours, honey.''

Angela grumbled under her breath, ''I have a dozen calls to make.'' Still she gathered some more flatware and started back to the kitchen.

''Let's walk outside,'' Zach said to Laura.

Surprised, she only nodded. ''I should really help Angela....''

''You can do them tomorrow. We take turns in this house.''

Getting up, she walked with Zach to the door. He held it open for her and then took her elbow and guided her down the steps, walking silently toward the corral.

Laura simply stared at the beauty. The lights outside their house were the only manmade illumination. Millions of stars silently looked down upon the earth as they did.

But on earth, despite being in the country, it was noisy. Crickets chirped, grasshoppers buzzed and the grass rustled in the soft cool breeze that blew. A cow mooed off in the distance, and Laura heard a horse snort and stomp its foot.

"Why do you think Angela is following in her mother's footsteps?"

Zach looked up at the sky, a look of sudden pain in his eyes. His hair ruffled as the wind gusted. "We're going to have rain tomorrow."

"How can you tell?"

"You can smell it in the air, feel it in the current. The wind is coming from the southwest. That time of year. Next few hours and the stars will be blocked out and it'll be so bleak, empty, no light at all...desolate."

Laura looked around trying to imagine what it would look like with no light at all. She wasn't sure she could.

"But I like it. There is a peace out here. Roots, Laura. I fought and scraped to save this land. It means a lot, the friends around here mean a lot. The church. Desolate? I don't see it that way. Even in the darkness, you can still see God's wonderful work. But Carolyn never understood that. There weren't enough people for her. And Angela is the same way."

Zach shifted, propping a booted foot on the railing and facing her. "She wants out, away. She wants to climb mountains and reach for stars."

When he paused, Laura whispered softly, "And go into the medical field like her mother."

"She told you this." It was a simple statement. Nothing more, nothing less; just an acknowledgment of something.

"Is that really so bad?"

"Yes. No." A sigh escaped. "I don't know. Julian is a doctor, or will finish shortly and be one. But she wants emergency medicine. Then a week later she is going to be a horse trainer. She just can't make up her mind."

"I know. She's mentioned horse training, too. You know, Zach, it's not that abnormal for a child her age to want different things from day to day. Maybe if you just let her explore with gentle guidance here and there, and lots of prayer, she'll hear God's voice and follow the path He's chosen for her."

Zach turned back, propping both arms on the fence.

Laura followed his example, moving closer. It seemed almost wrong to disturb the musical night with mere words. Whispering lowly, she continued, "Who knows, maybe she'll decide to be a vet."

"Gee, thanks," Zach said, chuckling.

"You're being too hard on yourself, Zach. You're being too hard on Angela. Relax. Let her grow up. She loves you very much. She's just searching is all."

"I'm trying, Laura. I really am."

Laura shivered.

She was surprised when Zach slipped an arm around her and rubbed her arm. "You're right. It's getting chilly. Let's get inside."

Laura was amazingly surprised at how much she enjoyed the warmth he offered and how much she just liked that arm around her. She knew she was being silly, but it felt good to be held.

Turning her toward the house, he started her back across the yard, sliding his hand down to her waist as he guided her. As they got to the steps, Zach slowed and released her. He urged her ahead of him and held the door for her.

Once inside he started toward the kitchen. "You'd best get to bed while I check up on my daughter."

"Okay," she said, deciding Zach was embarrassed after their talk. Turning, she started toward the hall.

"Oh, and Laura?"

She paused, turning back. He stood across the room, his hand on the kitchen door. "Thank you for talking."

A warm glow rose in Laura spilling out into a soft smile. "Anytime, Zach. Anytime. Oh, and Zach?"

"Yes?" he asked, his hand still on the door.

"There's a little something I'd like you to do for Angela tomorrow...."

Chapter Ten

"I can't believe I'm actually doing this."

Laura smiled at Zach. When she smiled like that it made him forget what he'd agreed to. Almost. She had a beautiful smile. The small half curve, the way she tilted her head slightly, the twinkle in her eyes. "It'll do you good to help your daughter shop."

"I don't know anything about girls' clothing."

"Women's," Laura corrected. "Your daughter is in adult sizes."

Zach shook his head, feeling helpless.

"Here she comes."

Zach turned and saw, sure enough, his

daughter was crossing the street, coming toward them. Watching her, the way she walked, the grin she tossed at a friend as she waved, Zach suddenly realized his little girl was indeed growing up.

"Uncle Mitch wasn't in. I told Betty I'd be back by later."

When had it happened? When had she suddenly gone from diapers and bottles to this young woman? "You ready to shop?" he asked.

Gone was the woman, and the grin that he knew so well returned. "Yeah!"

Or maybe the girl-woman were both her. "Great. Laura?" He turned, and saw the knowing look on her face. For someone who couldn't remember, she sure did act like she did.

"I'm ready."

Shaking his head, he motioned toward the shop down the street. Zach trailed along behind them, watching Angela's bouncy step as she headed toward the store. Laura walked more sedately, though her compact body spoke of a purpose as she walked along.

After going into the store with the two

women, he watched as they shopped. They went up and down the aisles, holding up short dresses, long dresses, sleeveless dresses, dresses with sleeves to their wrists. They held up odd patterns and bold, bright, vibrant colors. Neither Laura nor his daughter were interested in his opinion that he thought Angela looked best in pastels.

All in all, Angela ended up convincing him to buy a bold red top, a new pair of jeans and a beautiful short white dress with a jacket dotted with occasional sequins. Of course, she had to have shoes, but after they found some and when they went toward the intimate apparel, he parted from them.

"Zach?"

He simply shook his head. "Sorry, Laura. This isn't something I know how to do." He could feel the heat climbing up his cheeks. When Laura grinned, he allowed a slow grin to spread across his face in return. Ambling over to her, he slipped an arm around her and pulled her close.

Laura's eyes widened in shock.

He leaned down and bussed her on the cheek.

"Daddy!"

Laura blushed.

He released her and winked at his daughter. "I didn't want to be the only red one here. Now, go shop."

He couldn't believe he escaped unscathed, leaving a gaping Laura and a giggling daughter behind.

Life could be good sometimes, he thought, as he sauntered through the store, thinking he had an idea of just what he wanted to do. He just might decide to court that little lady there.

Yes, indeed. Memory or no memory, he found her attractive.

"He finds you attractive," Angela whispered.

Laura turned from where she stood staring after Zach. "No. He can't."

Confusion crossed the young girl's face. "My daddy is supposed to be handsome. All the women in town talk about him. And he's not married. Why can't he like you?"

Laura turned. "I mean, well…honey, I have a big gaping hole where my memory should be."

"You don't like him?"

Laura simply looked at Angela.

Angela giggled again. "You do like him!"

Laura groaned. "Come on, let's find you undergarments for this dress."

"Can I tell you something, Laurie?"

Angela bounced alongside her, holding the dress up, examining it, turning it, totally ignorant of the people she nearly ran over in her intense desire to study her new dress.

"Sure, Angie," Laura returned.

Grinning, Angela cocked her head and cut her eyes at Laura. "Harry kissed me."

Finally dropping the dress into the cart she hurried over and started browsing the undergarments holding them up, sizing them then discarding them for others.

"Ah, Harry. Isn't that a little soon?"

"All the girls do it, and he is a nice guy and I just really like him. But don't worry. I know better than to do anything else. Daddy raised me right and gave me the talk."

"It's more than that. I mean, your daddy's opinion is important, but there is someone else...."

"I know." Angela found the appropriate

sizes and dropped them in the baskets. "I'm a Christian. I know it'd be displeasing to God for me to do something like that. I don't like hurting God's heart."

Hurting God's heart. Laura thought that a beautiful description of what you did to your heavenly Father when you sinned. "Yeah. Just like you don't like hurting your daddy's heart, either?"

Angela shrugged. "I just don't know how to talk to him. He only orders. He doesn't know how to talk."

The frustration changed Angela's face back into a little girl's, wreathed with confusion and pain. Tenderly, Laura reached out and brushed a strand of Angela's hair back. "I think he's trying. I imagine he's been so involved in work and responsibilities that fun got dropped by the wayside. What do you say to us teaching him about fun?"

Angela grinned, her eyes growing wide, and sparkling. "Oh, cool! Like what?"

Seeing the joy on the young girl's face, she cautioned. "Now, we may not be able to get to him at first, but if we keep working, he just might come around."

"Yeah."

"And you have to be careful, not to get upset but continue to encourage him."

"I don't get mad."

She said it so seriously that Laura had to laugh. "Oh, of course not. You're exactly like your daddy. And he never gets angry, either."

"So, tell me what I have to do."

Laura proceeded to do just that.

Chapter Eleven

"So, where's our Laura? I thought you said she'd be right along?"

Zach shrugged. "Women. You know how they are. I have no idea. They said it'd take five minutes."

Zach stood and walked across Mitch's office to look out the window. The trees were all in bloom, and people strolled lazily along the sidewalks doing their daily chores. But no signs of Laura or Angela.

Angela. She had certainly changed over the past few weeks. "I swear, Mitch, you should see the way Angela has opened up to Laura. If she's an hour longer I'm not going to complain. Angela is finally talking to me without a scowl on her face. I'm not sure what Laura did. But she did something right."

"Yeah, I'd say she did."

Mitch's eyes gleamed with amusement. Zach scowled. "Get that look off your face, little brother."

Mitch opened his mouth to reply when the buzzer on his desk buzzed. Going over, he snagged up the receiver. "Yeah, Betty?"

"Uh, could your brother step out here a moment, sheriff?"

Mitch glanced up with a questioning look. Zach shook his head.

"Sure. He'll be right out."

"Think Angie-girl did something and doesn't want her Uncle Mitch to know?" Mitch asked.

Zach groaned. "I hope not."

He stood and headed out the door toward the front office.

"Nah." Mitch chuckled, following. "If she'd done something wrong, she'd be waiting for me to come to her instead of you."

Zach shot his brother another look before walking out into the lobby. He met Betty's grinning features along with two other deputies of Mitch's. "What's going…"

"Hold it right there, mister."

Hearing Laura's voice, Zach turned and came face-to-face with a scene right out of the 1800s—almost. The only thing that didn't look right about it was the water pistol.

"Nice mask you got there, Laura," Zach drawled, shifting his weight to one hip. "Mind telling me what you're doing with a handkerchief over your mouth and nose?"

"Hands up."

She poked him with the gun.

Zach shook his head.

"We're kidnapping you, Daddy."

Zach turned and saw Mitch standing, hands in the air, grinning patiently—while his daughter held a water gun in his back. "Angie?"

Except Angela's water gun was much bigger with a big tank attached like a flamethrower. She also had on Mitch's cowboy hat and a handkerchief so only her eyes showed.

"Looks like I'm a hostage, big bro. You'd better go with them or they might get violent.

And I sure don't want this uniform to get all wet.''

One of the deputies snickered.

Zach turned back around.

The deputies looked to the ceiling.

"And I thought you were a good influence for my daughter," Zach muttered just loud enough for his captor to hear.

"Aww, come on, play along," she whispered. In a louder voice, she said, "Now get your hands up." She poked him again, and he reluctantly stuck his hands in the air. "Two hours of time is all we want. Otherwise, we make you look like you've reverted to a two-year-old and wet your pants."

The entire office burst into laughter.

Mitch slapped Zach on the shoulder. "She's got you there."

"Yeah. Okay, okay. I give in."

Shooting a look at his daughter, he muttered, "We'll talk later."

"Can I spend the night with you, Uncle Mitch?" Angela asked, giggling.

"Don't get me in on this. I'm only a hapless victim."

Laura motioned toward the door. "Come on. You can drive."

"Where are we going?" Zach asked, ambling toward the door, hands still in the air. "To rob a bank?"

"What do you think, Angie-babe? Should we rob it?"

"In a town this small?" Angela shook her head. "No way, boss. I say we take him out to the…" She broke off and chuckled.

"Shush, girl, before you give it away. We don't want *them*—" she motioned to Mitch "—to find the body."

"Go on, Zach. I know this county. If you don't show up tomorrow I'll make a thorough search."

"Stop encouraging them," Zach growled, though there was no heat in his voice. As a matter of fact, he was rather enjoying listening to his daughter's laughter and watching the mischievous sparkle in Laura's eyes.

"Talk to you later, Mitch."

"Yeah, bro. Sure."

They started out of the station but didn't make it past the door. Harry came bounding in and ran right into Laura.

Laura tumbled, dropping the water pistol.

Zach reacted, springing to catch her.

Angela squeaked and stumbled back, spraying water everywhere.

"What's going on!" Harry hollered, falling back from the water that hit him right square in the face.

"You okay, Laura?" Zach asked, holding her firmly.

"I'm fine. I'm fine. Really," Laura said, and pulled away.

Relieved, Zach released her, ignoring the laughter, the sputtering coming from Harry, the ribbing Mitch was doing. Instead he watched the woman blush and reach down for her gun.

She was something else. The entire town would be talking about this for a long time to come, he imagined.

"I don't even want to think what people are going to be saying about this," Zach muttered to Mitch who was still laughing.

"That the sheriff was held hostage?" He hooted with laughter.

Zach started to retort when he realized

Laura still hunkered over her gun, not moving, her hand on the water pistol.

"Laura?"

She didn't budge. Nor did she answer.

The noise died down, and Mitch moved forward. Zach stopped him with a hand on his arm. "Laura?" he said again, softly.

When she still didn't answer, he reached down and touched her.

She exploded into motion, jumping up and turning, gun pointed right at him, eyes wide with terror.

Harry started forward.

"No," Mitch said, authoritatively.

"Laura." Zach said firmly, willing her to hear. *Father, what is going on? Help,* he silently prayed. Every single person in the office was on their feet, antsy at the implied threat in Laura's stance. What had been funny and a game only moments ago was now a serious situation that might just be turning dangerous.

Zach didn't believe that, but knew the others didn't know Laura as well as he did. "It's okay," he said to Mitch. "It's all right,

Laura. It's me, Zach.'' He held out a hand reaching for her, his eyes never leaving hers.

Her eyes slowly cleared and focused on him. ''I—what happened?''

''You tell us.'' He touched her hand that she unconsciously held out and enclosed it in his bigger one. Her hand was like ice.

''Is she okay, Daddy?'' Tentatively, nervously, unsure, his daughter's voice drifted to him from Mitch's side.

Zach moved forward and slipped an arm around Laura. ''She's fine, darlin','' he said even though everyone could see Laura was as pale as the moon against the ink-black sky. Discreetly he nudged Laura with his arm, turning her as he turned his own body. Smiling, he said, ''And I promise to go with you two and submit to your nefarious plans. But I left something in Uncle Mitch's office. Just let me get it.''

Keeping his arm firmly around the woman who still appeared ready to faint at the least provocation, he led her down the hall, leaving Mitch behind to run interference.

Pushing open the door to the office, he guided Laura in. ''Close the door, Angela.''

He moved to a bench and seated himself, automatically pulling Laura next to him. Holding her close he said, "Okay, out with it. What happened out there, darlin'?"

Laura trembled against him, her entire being shaking with aftershock. Icy cold hands inched up his chest and clutched his shoulders. Her rapid breathing hit his neck. His heart ached for her.

"I—I—"

"Angela honey, get Laura some water."

She nodded and hurried out of the office. "Come on, Laura," Zach's voice crooned gently. "It's okay."

Laura lifted her frightened gaze to his. His body was warm, steady, safe. The arms around her held her firmly and his eyes radiated a gentleness in them, a willingness to listen.

She didn't want to let go of him. She wanted to sink into the aura of safety that shone so promisingly in his eyes.

Another part of her, however, slowly took control, calming her, easing the fear and forcing her into a matter-of-fact facade.

This state felt familiar somehow. Though

raging on the inside, her outer demeanor appeared suddenly peaceful and professional. Meeting those deep, dark eyes, she stated quite simply, "I think someone tried to kill me that night on the road."

She saw the look of disbelief and shock on his face. Then his emotions were wiped clean, and he hugged her close. She didn't tell him how much that hug meant, how good it felt, how secure and warm. Instead, she simply leaned there against his chest, soaking in the warmth.

"Why do you think that?" he asked after stroking her back gently.

Laura shook her head, knowing he was going to think her crazy when she told him.

"It's okay," he murmured and rubbed her back again. The soothing tone, the way he stroked her back, felt wonderful and went a far way to alleviating her internal fear.

"Maybe I was wrong."

Zach wouldn't accept that. She could tell in the way his body stiffened, the way he held her tighter, the way he whispered, so low, "Talk to me, Laura. What did you remember?"

The musky scent of men's aftershave wrapped around her, relaxing her as much as the gentle cadence of his voice convinced her to confide in him. "Nothing, exactly," she said softly before saying, with a stronger voice, "I went to pick up the gun and smelled gasoline. All around me. There was pain and an urgency. Then it seems like..." She rubbed her head. "I think someone shot me."

Zach hugged her close.

Laura dropped her arm, going willingly back into his embrace. The residual terror of remembering someone or the feeling of being shot, she wished she could remember exactly but to think about it brought on pain.

"Laura, honey, you weren't shot. True, you were pretty beat up when you came in. But they didn't find any bullet holes in you."

She knew it sounded ridiculous so she dropped it. Besides, maybe he was right. All she remembered was the thought she was going to die. Why she associated that with a bullet she wasn't sure. "Am I losing my mind?"

"No, Laura. You're simply remembering something about guns. Maybe either you were shot in your past, someone you knew was, or you triggered something awful by picking up the water gun.''

Laura tried hard to recall, but the pounding in her head increased. ''I just don't know!''

''Here's your water, Laurie,'' Angela said hurrying in. Mitch was right behind her.

His dark eyes traveled over her before he shut the door. ''What's up?''

Realizing she was still on Zach's lap she tried to slide off. Zach's arms stayed firm for a moment before releasing her.

Oddly enough, she missed his embrace when she stood. Running a hand through her hair, she sighed. ''I don't know. I had some sort of flashback.''

''Anything to help us identify you?''

She shook her head. ''I don't think so.''

Mitch nodded and strolled over to lean against his desk. ''Feel up to fingerprinting now?''

''Yes.'' She definitely wanted that. Anything to give her a hint of who she was. She didn't like the flashes of memories she was having. She wanted to know who she was, just what she was, why a gun felt so familiar yet terrifying in her hand.

"Good," Mitch said, grinning.

"Does she have to have this done right now? Her burns might get infected," Angela said.

Feeling more herself, Laura smiled at Angela. "I'll be fine."

Taking the water, she lifted it and drank down a sip to satisfy the young girl who hovered near her elbow.

"Angela, can you show her where the fingerprint room is?"

"Sure. Come on, Laurie."

"Of course, *Angie.*"

Angela giggled. Zach smiled.

Laura paused long enough to send Zach a smile filled with gratitude and warmth before leaving.

Zach watched the two women leave the office.

"So what happened?" Mitch asked as soon as Laura was gone.

"Like she said, she had some sort of flashback. She thinks someone shot her. Mix that in with the smell of gasoline she said she experienced. I'm not sure what it meant.''

Mitch frowned. ''There wasn't any sign of bullets. Until now we've been certain it was a hit-and-run by a drunk. Wonder if there is anything to her story.''

''Did the doctor find any evidence of something like that?'' Zach was horrified to think someone might have actually tried to hurt Laura. Horrified and starting to get angry.

Mitch shook his head and moved around the small wooden desk to sit down in his chair. A loud creak sounded as he sat before turning to the computer and pulling up the file on Laura. ''All we have here is multiple lacerations, contusions, some bad muscle tearing according to the doctor's report. Let's see, she had stitches in her left arm two different places, one leg and her head in two spots. Those were all taken out before she left the hospital. The doctor also told me personally he doesn't know how she kept from breaking bones in such a mess. Then of course, there were the multiple burn spots, the worst ones on her hands, which suggests she grabbed on

to something hot when she pulled herself out
of the car.''

Zach shuddered, memories of old as well
as his new ones with Laura swirling inside
him. He knew Laura was having nightmares
and wondered how long those would go on.
His wife hadn't had a chance to have nightmares. She'd never regained consciousness.
''I just can't imagine...''

Mitch turned to face Zach. ''That's just
what the doctor is guessing. Will found her
outside the car, unconscious, bloody and
burned. If someone else had pulled her out
before leaving the scene her hands probably
wouldn't be burned. And I've got to tell you,
Zach, I saw the car. A small, compact size, it
went up hot. The gas tank must have somehow leaked and caught fire. It rolled, ended
up against a tree. The window that was open
enough for her to fit out was totally black.
Actually, the entire car was. But she had to
wiggle through there, and in the shape she
was in when they brought her in, only someone with a strong will would have been able
to make it. God was certainly on her side or

she would have burned to death in that mangled heap of steel.''

"I don't like this at all." Zach scowled.

Mitch crossed his hands over his stomach and leaned back. "Neither do I. But, Zach?''

Zach glanced up at his little brother. "Yeah?''

"If I were you, I wouldn't take this lightly. I'd keep an eye on her. We don't know anything about her. She could be on the other side of the law just as easily as this side.''

Zach wanted to protest, loudly, but knew Mitch was only being a good sheriff warning him of a very real possibility. "I don't believe that,'' he said mildly.

Mitch smiled. "Nor do I. But she does know how to handle a gun. It makes you wonder.''

Zach stared at his brother and thought, yeah, it sure does. And he certainly did plan to keep an eye on her. After all, he was attracted to her, he had a teenaged daughter. And good or bad, he wanted to get to know her better. Starting with finding out just what those two had been up to earlier.

Chapter Twelve

"This was what you wanted to do?"

Angela giggled, drawing a smile from Laura. She had to agree with Angela. Zach's look was priceless. He was totally bewildered. "You don't like a picnic? Ours didn't get finished, so we thought..."

Zach shook his head. "I haven't been here in years."

"I know, Daddy, but Laurie said you'd love it. Are you surprised?"

Laura watched as Zach's eyes scanned the small forest area before his lips quirked. "Yeah, squirt. I love it."

"Dad-dy!" Angela groaned at yet another

one of his nicknames for her. Laura enjoyed watching the two when they were getting along. They interacted so wonderfully. "You have to come see everything we have planned."

Angela wiggled out from behind the wheel and headed toward the back of the truck leaving Laura in the middle seat. It'd been a long drive out there, sitting next to Zach. The musky smell of Zach totally wrapping around her, the warmth of him so close, the feeling of safety he projected to her. And the attraction she felt, the need just to lean into him and hold him, be comforted and offer comfort. It had been quite disconcerting to experience all of this while Angela was gaily chatting away a mile a minute, oblivious.

Zach's hand touched her arm tentatively and he said low, his sweet gentle voice sliding into her and reminding her of just how attractive she thought this man was, "I never thought I had time for this. But seeing the excitement when she drove us out here convinced me I was wrong."

Laura glanced from the warm gentle hand to the deep dark eyes which gazed so steadily down at her. "She's still a kid in many ways."

"Thank you, Laura."

Smiling, she nodded. As she did, she noticed a hint of beard. Dark stubble showed from just beneath the surface of his skin. He probably had to shave twice a day to stay clean shaven.

Zach's hand trailed down her arm to her hand. "Laura, you know—"

"Come *on*, Daddy!"

And just like that, the spell was broken. Laura realized they weren't alone out here, this man wasn't interested in her. She was simply feeling the emotions most teenagers felt. And she was definitely not a teenager! She wished, however, Zach had finished what he was going to say. The consternation in his eyes as Angela came running back was priceless.

"We're coming, Angie," Zach said, and with one last odd look tossed at Laura, he climbed out of the truck.

Laura wasted no time clambering out the other side. She actually was out and around the truck before he was completely out of his side. Of course, he had to grab the rifle and picnic basket out of the vehicle.

"A swing?" His voice slipped up into a question of disbelief.

Angela giggled and nodded. "We found it when we were taking care of Jingle Bells. In the loft of the barn."

Zach nodded, then shook his head, before he finally nodded again. "We'll tie it up on one of those trees—"

"I'll do it!" Angela turned and sprinted off.

"Feel like you're in a whirlwind?" Zach drawled, watching helplessly as his daughter ran off.

Laura walked over and appropriated the picnic basket so Zach could get the cooler of drinks. "She has so much energy and life. I really enjoy her, Zach."

"She sure has changed since you've been around."

"I don't know about that. I have a feeling she was bored. She's enjoying teaching me about animals right now. She thoroughly loves it."

"Well, you have conquered the chicken coop."

They started walking toward a nearby shade tree, watching as Angela scampered up the tree like an agile monkey and set about tying the ropes to a large branch of the oak.

"I learned to use the water gun."

Zach set the cooler down and then leaned the rifle against a nearby tree. "What do you mean by that?"

Laura chuckled. "I take the water gun with me. If any of the chickens even look like they're heading for the gate or me, for that matter, I squirt them."

Zach simply stared in amazement.

Laura beamed. She was so proud of her accomplishment.

Zach had never heard of anyone using a water pistol....

"Well?" she prodded.

Zach chuckled, smiling warmly at the woman. "If it works, that sure is a good way to handle them, I'd say. Now, help me get this paraphernalia distributed so we can eat. I, for one, am hungry."

Laura's eyes twinkled, reminding him of

the morning glories blooming bright and full each day. She snatched the cloth out of the basket and sent it flying with a snap, laying it out on the ground. "There we go."

Laura flopped down on the ground and started setting out the food.

"I'm ready here, Dad. I want you to swing me later."

Zach grinned. "If you push me, too," he called up to his daughter.

She giggled and then swung down out of the tree. "Guess what I bought while we were in town?"

Reaching in her pocket she pulled out a bottle. "Nail polish."

Zach frowned. "I didn't know you wore nail polish."

"I don't. But Ha— Um, well, some friends said it looks nice on girls so I thought I'd wear some."

Zach's frown deepened, and Laura realized he was upset. "Harry's too old for you, Angela."

Angela's smile turned downward, her hands going to her hips. "Everyone dates people that old, Daddy."

Zach's hands went to his hips, imitating Angela's actions. "If everyone drove off the Simpson Cliffs, would you, too?"

"You always say that!" Angela's eyes filled with tears.

Laura, watching the two, decided to interrupt. "Will you paint my toenails, Angela, after we eat?"

Zach and Angela both turned, wearing identical frowns. She was amazed how much the two looked alike at this moment. Smiling weakly at Zach she silently pleaded for him not to ruin the afternoon. His frown faded and he turned to Angela. "You can wear the nail polish. But a date with Harry is out of the question."

"Daddy!"

"He compromised, honey. That's what being an adult is all about. Why don't you compromise now?"

"But Harry likes me," Angela said, and Laura could hear the note in her voice that said, *no one else will if I don't go out with him.*

Evidently Zach did, too. Laura could see him reach for and find some more patience.

"Okay, sweetheart, here's the deal. If you behave and I feel I can trust him, you can go with Harry to the end of the year dance. How's that?"

"But we have a dance next weekend."

"I'm not giving in on this, Angela. He's four years older than you. If you were eighteen that wouldn't matter. But you are fifteen. So it's compromise with me or forget it."

Angela bubbled with resentment then she nodded and flopped down. "Okay."

Silence fell as Zach seated himself. No words passed as all three filled their plates. They said a prayer and then began to eat.

Laura hurt for both of them. True, they had been totally uncommunicative and had made some progress. But she could see it in them, two people, trying to communicate, but not knowing how to go about it.

"So, will you paint my toenails, Angela?" she asked, having to break the silence somehow and unable to come up with another idea.

It worked. Angela glanced up, surprised, as did Zach. "You really want me to?"

Laura grinned. "Sure. And I'll paint yours if you want."

Angela's anger faded and she smiled. "I don't want my toenails painted. But I do want my hands. Will you help me with that, Laurie?"

Laura beamed with pleasure. "I'd love to."

The tension was gone. Laura was so relieved. "You know, Daddy, the spring festival next weekend, we're supposed to ride horses again. Can Miss Laurie ride with us? She's learning to ride Jingle Bells."

Laura choked on her sandwich. "No, really," she wheezed out thinking, *I just said I'd do anything to bring these two together. I don't think so.*

Zach reached over and pounded her on the back, which wasn't much help as now she couldn't breathe as well as was choking.

"No, Daddy, really she is. It'd be so cool if she could ride with us. Everyone would see what a good trainer I am."

"I'm fine, fine," Laura whispered, certain if she looked down she'd see her backbone where her ribs once were.

Zach immediately ceased his pounding. Frowning at Laura, he began to run his hand up and down her back. "I don't know, Angie. I don't think Laura likes riding horses."

Laura was about to object to his punishing help, but the switch to gentle strokes along her back made her forget completely what she was going to say. That felt good. Really good. She found herself relaxing and smiling.

"Sure she does. She takes lessons every day."

Laura's eyes drifted closed as the warm hand stroked up and down her back, pulling out all the stress she'd felt over the past weeks, making the problems fade, making her feel cared for. She heard Zach murmur something and Angela reply. Then Zach murmured something else. She could tell simply because his voice radiated down his arm, filling her with a simple feeling of warmth and calm.

"Don't you, Miss Laurie?"

"Hmm?" Laura opened her eyes to find Angela staring at her earnestly, and Zach staring at her like she...oh, dear.

A dull flush spread across her cheeks as she pulled away. "Of course I do, Angie."

Angie grinned. "Told you," she said to her daddy. To Laura she said, "That's great! I'll have Jingle Bells ready for you to ride next Saturday.'' Jumping up, she grabbed the rifle and went off into the bushes. ''Be right back.''

''I...what, Jingle Bells?'' Laura knew she sounded like a complete fool. However, she had no idea what she'd agreed to.

Zach's low chuckle worried her.

''What?'' she asked coolly.

His grin was infectious. ''Laura, my dear, you just agreed to ride with us next Saturday. And I could swear you don't like that horse.''

Laura wasn't about to admit she didn't know what she'd agreed to. ''She's growing on me,'' she muttered.

Leaning forward, Zach whispered, ''If I didn't know better, Laura, I'd say my touch was affecting you.''

The low drawl sent shivers down her spine. ''Not at all.'' No way would she admit to that, either.

Zach reached up, cupping her cheek. ''Oh?''

Laura melted.

Zach's eyes dropped to her lips and Laura couldn't help but wonder just what it'd be like to be held and kissed, wrapped in his arms in a close embrace....

He moved closer, his lips touching hers. "Oh, Zach," she whispered, and then sank into the kiss. It was everything and more. Joy, peace, completion, warmth.

Zach pulled back and lifted her hand and kissed her palm. "We'll take it one step at a time, Laura."

Laura sighed at the warm touch of his lips. She felt tears touch her eyes. "I just don't know who I am." With a watery chuckle, she continued, "Maybe the awkwardness between us will be gone now."

Zach shook his head. "Honey, I'll never push you. But if you think I'm completely calm, think again." Leaning forward he tenderly caressed her lips before releasing her.

Laura was breathless. "Right."

Zach nodded, grinning. "Like I said, something's here. I don't know what, Laura. And I won't push. But the time for ignoring it is over. I realized that today, riding all the way out here sitting next to you."

Laura laughed nervously.

He nodded. "Exactly. So, instead of pretending anymore let's just take it one day at a time, work together to get your memory back and then go from there. Okay?''

Laura was afraid she'd agree with anything at the moment just to get he conversation over. "It sounds wonderful.''

Zach shook his head. ''No, it doesn't. I'm not sure I like this much better than you. I like you, don't get me wrong, but I certainly wasn't looking for anything more than some-one for Angela.''

"You're great with flattery, Zach. Keep it up.''

Zach flushed. ''That's not what I meant. I'm too old for this.'' He chuckled and Laura joined in, the tension easing. When the chuckles died down, he continued, ''Anyway, what I meant was, I wasn't looking for a re-lationship. My mind has been centered on just getting my brothers raised and then my daughter. One day, later, in the future some-time, maybe then I thought there might be something. But not now.''

Laura took pity on him. ''Zach,'' she said softly. ''I know what you mean. I feel it, too. And yes, I panic, but simply because when you touch me, when you're near me I feel like there is a live current between the two of us. I'm just so afraid it's because I can't remember and am clinging to you. I'd hate to *wake up* and realize I hurt you by being something that I'm not right now.''

Zach looked at her and said, slowly, softly, ''I don't think you could ever do that, Laura.''

''Okay, you gonna push me, Daddy?'' Angela came wading back through the brush, rifle cradled closely.

Zach gave Laura one last look and stood. ''Sure thing, honey. Then we'll see about swimming....''

''Or painting toenails,'' Angela said.

''If you wait until we get home I'll give you a pedicure,'' Laura suggested.

Angela giggled. ''Promise?''

''Promise,'' Laura said.

Zach glanced back at Laura.

With a chuckle, he went over to where Angela was and began pushing her on the swing, talking and laughing.

Laura sat back and watched and thought how lucky she was to be part of such a wonderful family for however long it lasted.

Chapter Thirteen

She was going to get her revenge if she got a chance. No two ways about it. "Time to learn about stable duty," she muttered. "You should know everything if you're going to be riding Jingle Bells in the small parade," she continued.

Laura shoveled Jingle Bells' stall out, continuing to glare at the horse, whom she'd tied just outside the cubicle. "You could do this out in the corral or in the fields, you know."

The horse shook its head and snorted at her, which reminded Laura too much of a laugh.

"I am certain whatever I did before I lost

my memory, it had nothing to do with this. Of course, I imagine any horse would be easy to clean up after except you. Not that I'd want to. I'm beginning to think I don't like horses.'' Laura didn't mention she was irked because she'd never managed to stay on the horse more than five minutes at a time, nor was she yet able to mount it without help. And now to have the horse smirking at Laura like she had the upper hand. Laura had a feeling Jingle Bells didn't let people or animals get the upper hand where she was concerned.

Laura finished shoveling and moved out of the stall, pausing to rub her back. She could hear talking off in the distance, men laughing, and the ever present sound of wind, carrying the smell of mesquite on its wings.

''I now have a new respect for Angie, that she insists on taking care of you all alone.''

Laura bent down and grabbed the handles of the wheelbarrow. ''Believe me, though, after this parade, I'm going to back out gracefully from ever riding you again.''

Laura lifted.

A blunt object hit her right in the rear and

she went headfirst right into the wheelbarrow. "Agh!"

Tumbling out, she rolled over and glared at the horse who pawed the ground with her foot and tried to look superior as she turned her head away.

"Ugh, ugh!" Laura raked her face. "Gross, gross, gross!"

Getting up she glared at the horse. "That's it. That is it! I have had it with you. You should be turned into dog food. Do you know that?"

The horse neighed at her.

She stomped forward and quickly untied the horse and dragged it into the stall.

The horse took its time.

"Nasty animal," she muttered.

Shoving the gate closed she glared again. "If Angela didn't love you..."

Shaking her head, she turned and went into the other part of the barn, closing the door behind her. Going to the sink, she turned it on full blast and started scrubbing her face and hair. As she scrubbed, Laura decided she and the horse had the same problem. They both wanted to be in charge.

"I must have been stubborn before," she mused. "I like to be in charge. That horse has got to give in sooner or later."

Grabbing the soap she started on her neck and arms. "And Zach." She smiled softly. "He is gorgeous, though I think he likes to be in charge, too. Of course, I don't mind it from him. At least he's reasonable and will compromise. Or he has so far. After talking with him the other day I really wish my memory were back." Fear rose up in her. Whispering to God, she said, "Then again, maybe I don't want to know."

A peace from within wrapped itself around her, easing her fears, reminding her that all things work together for those who love the Lord.

"Every day here at the house, his whole attitude is loving, caring, gentle—a protector," she whispered. "If only I could remember, find out just what's going on, who and what I am."

Sighing, she stood and turned off the water. "Nevertheless, I have no choice but to wait. Guide me, Father, show me what to do, which direction to take because I'm lost."

Laura sighed and then took time to gather her thoughts before finally turning. When she turned, though, it was to totally lose track of everything as she stared in stunned shock. "And the barn door is smoking," she whispered, looking at the wisps of smoke rising from the outside door.

Rushing forward, she touched the door and found it hot. "Oh, no..."

A shout went up in the other room. The stables! She could get out that way. She turned, and that's when she saw the smoke there, too.

Laura looked around, but the entire structure was going up around her, with no escape. She had to get out, but how?

"So you didn't find out a thing?" Zach asked in disbelief. He looked from Harry to Mitch. "Fingerprints didn't turn up anything?"

"Her hands were too scarred," Harry said, scowling. "It's not our fault, Zach."

Running a weary hand over his neck, Zach sighed. "Yeah, yeah. I know." Turning from the work he had been doing, he headed back up to the house and entered. "Give me five minutes to clean up and I'll be right with you.''

Going down to his room, Zach stripped, washed up quickly and put on fresh clothes. As he did he had to wonder what to do next for Laura. He looked out the window, and saw his daughter crossing the yard. And Harry standing there waving. No sign of Laura.

Though seeing Harry around his daughter put him in a bad mood, he had to grin at Laura's predicament. Yes, he'd been rotten to have her clean out the stables. But she'd been begging for something to do. He'd go out there right after he finished talking to Mitch and apologize. He'd figured she would have objected. She was one stubborn woman.

''Thinking about our mystery woman?''

Zach turned to see his brother standing in the doorway grinning. ''Yeah, as a matter of fact, I was.''

Zach walked out of the room and back down the hall to the kitchen where he poured himself some tea. Mitch helped himself to a glass and sat down at the table.''

Zach sighed. ''Her fingerprints were useless. She's not remembering anything, at least not anything significant. I'm wondering if there is anything else we can do to figure out who she is."

"As a matter of fact, Zach, that's one of the reasons we came out here today. Harry is going to take a picture that we can send out to other authorities. We'll see if anyone can match her up with information they have."

"She's not a criminal."

"I'm not saying she is, Zach. But the woman can handle a gun like a professional. You said so yourself. And she's not quite..."

Zach watched his brother hesitate, his brow furrowing.

"I can't put my finger on it, but she's not normal."

"What are you getting at, Mitch?"

"I don't know, big bro. I only wish I did. But you tell me how many people handle a gun as well as she does, seems as sharp and quick as...as..." Shaking his head he sighed. "I think if we send out a picture on her, someone might eventually know her. Zach, she could be skeet champion in some town. You know people who practice with rifles and pistols like that all know each other. They participate in gaming and practices together.

Meetings, the range. It's slim, I admit it, but it is a chance. And if she does happen to have a record then just maybe they'll find that.''

"I guess anything is worth a shot at this point. She's still having nightmares.'' Zach scowled, feeling helpless. Last night again he'd heard whimpering and then a thud as she'd fallen out of bed. By the time he was up and dressed, she had gone outside, and he had no idea which direction she'd taken.

"You have any idea what these nightmares are about?''

"I think she's trying to remember something and has it blocked. The doctor said it was a possibility. But she did have a head injury and so he said it could also be from that. Laura has refused to drive to Chenyville and talk with the psychologist.''

Mitch nodded, resting his hands over his flat abdomen. "I'd heard—''

"Boss! Come quick! The barn's on fire!''

"What the—'' Zach began.

"Fire? How on earth could a fire erupt? It hasn't been *that* dry,'' Mitch said, tersely.

Shooting to his feet, Zach raced across the room to the front door, toward Harry's voice.

Mitch was right on his heels.

Zach slammed out onto the front porch and sure enough, there were flames leaping up around the base of the large red building.

"What happened?" Mitch snapped out.

Zach saw his men leading the last of the horses from the adjoining stables.

"I was on my way to see Miss Laura and snap a picture. I saw smoke and then, whoosh, the whole thing went up!" Zach noticed for the first time that Harry gripped a camera in his right hand.

"Laura..." Zach turned back, scanning the crowd as he took off down the steps. "Angela..."

"Daddy!"

Relief weakened Zach's knees as he saw his daughter running toward him.

"I can't find Laurie!"

"Zach, we got a problem. Look!"

Zach looked. His heart thudded to his feet. Laura stood in the second story of the barn, looking out, flames leaping around her, with no escape.

Chapter Fourteen

Thick clouds of dry suffocating smoke poured into the loft where Laura stood gasping and choking, trying to suck in enough air to breathe.

Below she saw people come running, saw Angela sprinting toward the house. Oh, good, Angela, she thought dimly. She had been worried about her. Dizzily she leaned against the wall and jerked on the window. If she could get it open, she could get out. She knew it.

The floor was warm, and Laura silently acknowledged she didn't have much time. Plus her brain had started getting foggy. She recognized the symptoms. She jerked again on the window—and that's when she saw Zach.

He stopped next to his daughter and stared up at where Laura stood, horror etching his features. "You lost your wife, didn't you Zach? Now you think you're going to watch someone else die."

Laura's eyes watered and burned. "Father, help me. I can't get it open," she whispered. Her lungs felt on fire, "I'm not dying! I've come too far. I'm not going to lose him! I have to find him," Laura cried out. "And I won't put Zach through that!" Glancing down she spasmed with a coughing fit.

That's when she saw the crowbar. Her answer! Staggering over, she grabbed the heavy piece of metal. The sound of the snapping flames, of beams falling, caving in terrified her, but she forced herself to calm. Now wasn't the time to panic. She was running out of air, fast. It was going to be a race to see if she ran out of air or was burned alive first.

And Laura didn't like those two options. Shoving back to her feet she made it to the window. Zach was below directing people. She saw Angela running toward her father, something in her arms. Then she met Zach's eyes. His mouth moved, telling her something, but she couldn't hear.

Laura shook her head, realizing she was drifting and forced herself to look at the bar in her hands. Lifting it was hard, it felt like it weighed a ton. She concentrated and then swung, putting her entire body behind her.

The crowbar hit the window, its impact reverberating all the way up her arms. The sound of shattering glass and the whoosh of air hit Laura's senses. So did the yelling below.

Focusing on the group below she realized they had run from the glass, but were now back and holding out a blanket, yelling at her to jump. Laura sucked in great gulps of air before nodding. She hit the window hard again, forcing the wood which had held the panes to break.

Then jerking off a shoe she worked to clear the sill of the rest of the glass. With the oxygen flooding into the room her head quickly cleared. She slipped one leg out and grabbed the sill, looking down.

"Jump, Laura!" Zach shouted, his face full of fear, worry, determination.

Laura started to nod when the floor fell out from underneath her. She grabbed the sill in shock and fear, pulling herself into the window. Flames and heat whooshed up, singeing her leg. Jerking her other leg through the window, she said quickly and loudly, "You said You'd have angels there to guard us lest we dash our foot against a stone. Help me God," and jumped.

Zach held tight to the blanket, his heart in his throat as Laura's body came barreling down toward them. He hadn't missed the flames leaping up behind her just as she'd jumped.

Laura hit the blanket. Muscles bulged as a couple of the men got knocked off-balance. Zach let go and snatched Laura before she had time to bounce a second time. Pulling her into his arms, he held her body close. "Are you okay?"

Laura wheezed but nodded.

"Get back! It's going to go!" Mitch yelled and grabbed Zach's arm, pulling him out of the way. Zach nodded gratefully to Mitch who also had an arm around Angela as they ran.

Zach heard the crash but didn't look back. "Mitch, can you handle this? I need to get her inside."

Laura clung to him as she wheezed in and out. Her hands clutched, unconsciously twisting his shirt as she hacked.

"Take it easy, honey. Just try to take slow breaths. You have plenty of air now. No more smoke."

Angela ran up the steps ahead of him and pulled open the door. She didn't ask questions. Zach had never been more proud of his daughter than he was as she followed him into the house. "Angie, go get me a wet cloth and some ice water."

Moving to the sofa, he lay his bundle down and then examined her, all the while crooning soft encouraging words. She smelled sharply of smoke and was a bit blackened in places, especially her right leg, but as best he could tell, she wasn't injured, except for the problem of breathing. Realizing his knees were knocking he dropped down on the sofa by her and cupped her cheek. "You're alive, honey. No damage."

Tears filled Laura's eyes. Zach couldn't handle that and hauled her into his arms and held her.

She started to sob, deep wracking sobs, trembling all over. Zach realized he was trembling just as much. What would he have done if Laura died? He'd gotten used to her musical laugh, the twinkle in her eyes, crossing swords with her in wit and her sharp mind. She'd done so much for Angela, and him, he suddenly realized. So much of his pain was gone. He had actually relaxed and learned to enjoy life.

Feeling the trembling body held so tightly in his embrace he came to a bone-shaking realization. He loved her.

He *loved* her.

He'd known he was attracted to her, but this—this deep abiding need to nurture, to spend the rest of his life with her—this was a shock.

"Here, Daddy," Angela said, rushing back in. He glanced up, saw the confusion on her

face as she observed him holding Laura. Zach
eased off on his hold.

"She's gonna be fine, Angie-doll. She just
has to release some emotion." He winked at
her.

He felt Laura work and win control over
her emotions and then pull back. "I'm fine,"
she whispered, breathing in and then coughing. "Really. Just somewhat rattled."

Angela sat down on the coffee table and
handed Laura the water. Zach helped Laura
take a sip as her hands were still unsteady.
So were his, for that matter. He was still trying to come to grips with the fact that he
loved this woman. He handed the glass back
to Angela and accepted the cloth and began
to wipe Laura's face and neck. "That feels
so good after the heat," she whispered.

Zach thought being near her felt pretty
good. With each stroke it was an affirmation
she was okay. As each streak of black was
removed, more and more of her was revealed,
and his heart slowed its fast beat.

Finally Laura nodded and pushed back in
complete control. Turning, she looked up at
Angela and smiled. She reached out, took his

daughter's hand and squeezed it. "Thank you. How is Jingle Bells?"

Zach blinked. She was worried about the horse she had been muttering about these past weeks?

"All the horses got out of the fire. They're working with them right now. Jingle Bells is okay. But I'd better go check and make sure none of the others are injured."

Zach listened to that and realized his daughter was so grown-up in many ways. Smiling he thought he was going to have to accept that and let go in some areas. "Good idea, darlin'," he said softly.

She jumped up and raced back outside.

Zach turned, focusing his gaze on Laura. "What happened? What were you doing up in the loft?"

Laura shook her head. "I didn't have much choice. The entire barn was in flames." She chuckled, which set off another round of coughing.

"We should take you to the doctor—"

"No! I'm fine. Really." She caught her breath.

"Why are you laughing?" Zach questioned, thinking it was probably leftover emotions.

A small smile touched her lips. "I had just asked God for direction, and I find it ironic that there was no choice but to go up. Makes me think God is trying to tell me to let Him guide me and handle the problems."

Zach grinned. "Okay, okay. I give up. You're not a normal female."

"Oh?" she asked, arching an eyebrow at him, her eyes twinkling with a spark of amusement.

"I'd expect most people to be falling apart, not chuckling over a parallel they've found in a prayer."

Laura sighed and dropped her feet to the floor. Leaning back against the couch she turned her gaze to Zach's. He saw the seriousness enter her eyes, the laughter die a quick death. "I should be falling apart. Zach, I didn't want Angie to overhear, but I am certain I smelled gasoline."

"What?" Alarmed, Zach gripped his legs to keep from grabbing her. "I don't store gasoline in the barn. Everyone knows better than to do that."

"No, no. I don't know if the smell was real or not. I smelled it just as I regained some memories. Or I think they're memories."

Reaching out, he took Laura's hand and clasped it. "What is it?"

He now knew why Laura had seemed glad that Angela was away. She wanted to tell him something and didn't want to alarm his daughter.

"I don't know, exactly. I was in a panic because there was smoke coming in under both doors. I saw the ladder and went up to the loft. The entire time I was praying. And I said that I had to find *him*. I wouldn't give up. Not until I found him."

"Who?"

Laura simply shook her head. "I didn't even realize I was saying it as I fought my way up the ladder and then to the window. It was only as you carried me in here that I remembered. Zach, it looks like I was on my way here searching for someone."

Her eyes turned dark with pain and worry. "And I think someone doesn't want me to find him."

Chapter Fifteen

"**Y**ou've got that right."

Zach and Laura both turned to see Mitch coming in, blackened with soot. Stomping his feet, he walked across the room. "Zach, that fire was set. So either whoever did it was after her, or it was simply more vandalism against you."

"You?" Laura looked in shock at Zach. "Why would someone have something out for you?"

Zach looked at Mitch with exasperation.

"I think she should know, Zach. It was her that nearly got her boots melted into soup out there."

Zach sighed. "Okay, okay. I just don't like others knowing my business. It's my problem and I'll solve it."

"What?" Laura asked, concerned at the harsh lines of frustration on Zach's face.

Mitch didn't wait for Zach to tell her. He sat down on the coffee table, clasping his hat and allowing it to dangle loosely between his knees. "It seems someone has been vandalizing our property out here. We've been finding dead cattle out on the range. One of our line shacks was burned, forcing us to move our cattle to another grazing field."

"We thought," Zach interrupted, "it might possibly be kids playing. But now with this, I'd say someone was serious."

"So this wasn't against me?"

"We don't want to rule that out," Mitch cautioned. "Let's just take this one step at a time. I think it was arson. We'll have someone out here to check it. In the meantime, the men are working to get things set up somewhere else and working on the last of the fire to keep it contained."

"Thanks, little bro," Zach said, and meant it.

The front door swung open and Harry walked in, stomping his feet before entering. "It looks like the worst of it is out, Sheriff, however, it's going to be smoldering for a while. It might be a good idea for someone to keep an eye on it. Red told me to relay that message."

"I'm sure he's already assigned someone," Zach said wryly. "The old coot is always one step ahead of me."

"Um, do you still want the woman's picture taken?"

Zach watched Laura rub her head in pain. Shaking his head, he said, "We'll do it at church, Sunday, if that's okay. That'll give her a bit of time to recover. Is that okay with you Laura?"

She nodded. "I don't know, my head is killing me. Three days will be fine."

Harry nodded to Mitch. "I'll be out in the vehicle."

When he left, Zach turned to Laura and urged her to lie down, tucking a sheet over her and laying a cloth over her head. "I want you to stay like this for a while or it's a trip to the doctor."

Laura didn't argue, which told Zach just how exhausted she was. However, she did reach out and capture his hand. He sat down next to her and whispered some soft words of comfort. Whether Miss Laura knew it or not, she was becoming quite dependent on him, he thought.

His brother cleared his throat.

Zach realized he was grinning and wiped the smile off his face.

Mitch's stretched into a grin with a very knowing look wreathing his features.

"Did you ever find the ghosts out on the ranch Zach was telling me about?"

It took a moment for Zach to realize Laura was asking Mitch the question.

"Oh. Well, no. But we do know it's no ghost." Mitch's smile faded, his brow furrowing into a frown. "We found tire tracks out that way. I guess our little old lady was right, and there have been people out on her ranch. And Zach, I was going to talk to you about this. It seems that those tracks lead in the general direction of the ranch here."

"Our pranksters?"

"Looks that way. Remember when that

photographer disappeared a while back? We thought he had drifted on? I'm wondering if he isn't involved in something here and just dropped out of sight.''

Zach realized Laura was snoring softly and gently tucked her hand under the sheet. Getting up he motioned to Mitch and moved over to the table in the dining area. ''Yeah, I seem to remember that. What was that kid's name? Michael? Morgan? Mark?''

''Mark. It would fit. Photographer out here in the middle of West Texas? And snooping around everywhere he shouldn't. He was even in my office a few times. Then you caught him out this way once.''

''Yeah. You know, Mitch, you might have something there. Keep me updated and I'll keep an eye out for anything odd.''

Mitch nodded at Laura. ''Keep a close eye on her, too. I'm not at all convinced that she isn't somehow involved. I just don't believe in coincidences.''

Zach nodded. ''I will. I suppose I should go out and check out how much damage we have.'' Zach ran a weary hand down his face. ''Between everything going on here and trying to juggle it with repairing my broken relationship with my daughter, I feel like I'm getting further and further behind.''

Mitch glanced out with *the look* in his eyes, as Zach had always called it.

''Go ahead, spit it out. You have something to say, and you aren't going to go until you do.''

Mitch shrugged. ''It seems to me you're making enough money now you could hire someone to handle the paperwork and someone to oversee some of the other areas you insist on handling yourself.''

Zach started to strenuously object, having always believed his business was his own responsibility. But, in the past few weeks, Laura had taught him something important— that he was losing a very precious gift without even realizing it. He was losing his daughter. He had determined he wouldn't lose her. And in the process, he was discovering the joy of being carefree again. Having time to spend with people and enjoy life.

How long had it been since he'd taken time to just stop and have a picnic? ''Maybe you're right, Mitch.''

Dumbfounded, Mitch gaped. "Since when?"

Zach shot him a look telling him what he thought of his shock. "I have realized lately that I haven't had a lot of time with my daughter or...to experience life." His gaze drifted to Laura who lay so still on his sofa.

"Ah, well, then, all I can say is God must have sent Laura in answer to Julian's and my prayers."

Zach glanced back at Mitch planning to deny it, but Mitch raised a hand. "Might as well admit it. It's written all over you. You love her. I'm not sure how I feel about that. I sure wish you'd waited until she got her memory back. But, I guess in this, we'll just have to trust God."

Zach fought what Mitch said before finally sighing. "Yeah. Heaven knows, Mitch, I don't want another woman in my life, or I didn't until I met Laura. She's healed my broken family and brought new life to us. She's brought new life to me, to a part I thought had died."

Mitch nodded. "Enough said. I'd better get on back to town so I can check some of this out. I'll have someone here later to confirm what I think. In the meantime, take care of Angela and keep her close to the house.''

Zach nodded and walked his little brother to the door. ''By the way, I got a letter from Julian. He'll be back here in a few months, all done up and ready to open up practice.''

Mitch's lips quirked. ''And just where is he going to open practice?''

''I heard Parkenson is retiring.''

''But that means both doctors will be gone from the clinic.''

''Yeah. Well, evidently the clinic is going to be funded by a supporter of the hospital here and work as an outreach. He's applied for the job there, and they're looking to hire a second doctor to assist him. Anyway, at least he'll be back home.''

Mitch shook his head. ''Home. Yeah. And to think we only wanted to get out of here as teenagers.''

''And you still do?'' Zach asked softly.

Mitch shrugged. ''What time is there for me here?''

''You make a life for yourself. Find a woman, marry, settle down.''

"I want more. Besides, I doubt there's any woman here who'd marry me," Mitch said seriously.

"You still have your eye on that schoolteacher don't you?"

"She's married, Zach. Of course I don't. I gave that up long ago."

Zach wasn't so sure about that. Mitch was obsessed with Mary Anne Milford. He'd said when he was ten years old he was going to marry her. It had nearly destroyed him when Mary Anne had married. Now all he talked about was getting out of town. "That's good. We'll talk about it later. Go on and we'll see you Saturday night at the dance."

Mitch snorted. "You, at the dance? I'd like to see that."

Zach grinned and said low, "Well you're going to, because this man is going to be watching one girl and courting another."

Mitch lifted an eyebrow and then hooted. Slapping his hat against his leg he snagged the door and strode out. "This I can't wait to see."

Zach thought, neither could he. But, having set his mind to it, he was determined to court

Miss Laura and let her know just what his intentions were.

Well, Father, God. Looks like I just might be marrying after all.... He shook his head and strode off toward the barn to check on the progress, wondering if courting her was going to be as difficult as convincing his daughter to stay away from that young deputy. He watched the deputy release his daughter's hand, get in the truck and leave.

His daughter shot him a guilty glance, hurried over to Jingle Bells and took off on the horse's back.

He'd have a chance to find out soon enough, he supposed, watching as his daughter rode off in a cloud of dust. *Father, please, show me how to break through this final barrier with my daughter. I just don't know how to reach her, to make her understand I am not trying to punish her for being like my former wife.*

Aren't you? he thought suddenly.

Zach vehemently denied it. He was only doing his best, after all. It was his duty to see that she grew up responsible, lived to see her children, got a sane job. He wouldn't allow her to run wild like Carolyn had. No way.

The voice faded and drifted off leaving him empty, alone, and somehow finding himself denying even more that he had done anything wrong.

"Boss?" Red said walking up. "I got the preliminary report on losses. You want it?"

Zach nodded and walked off with Red, his mind still on his daughter and the direction he wanted to take with her. Everything would be fine. He didn't have anything to worry about. Nothing at all.

Chapter Sixteen

"What do you mean you told Harry you'd go with him?" Zach asked, his eyes darkening with anger.

"Daddy! You said if I was good I could."

"I specifically remember telling you not this dance but the school one."

"But that one is a whole month away."

"I don't care. He's too old for you."

"But—"

Zach shook his head. "Darlin', even if I let you, it wouldn't be right now. Mitch thinks he has a lead on whoever has been destroying our property and because of that, he and Harry will be on call. What if he suddenly had to desert you at the party? Besides that, Laura is starting to remember things and I want you nearby.''

''You'll be there and so will Laurie. This isn't fair!''

Zach sighed impatiently. ''I've made up my mind. When this is all cleared up, then we'll see.''

Fresh tears sprang to Angela's eyes. ''You just don't want me to be like Mama. I know that's what it is.'' Turning, she ran out of the house.

''Angie—''

''Let her go, Zach.'' Laura laid a hand against his arm. ''She needs the time to dry her tears and get over the pain.''

Zach slumped and Laura slipped her arms around him, hugging him. ''She'll be okay, Zach. Just give it one day at a time.''

Zach hugged Laura close, holding her as pain struck his heart. ''I just don't know what to do, Laura. I don't want her making the same mistakes.''

''Are you so sure they're mistakes?'' she asked softly. ''From what I've heard, Carolyn was irresponsible and lied to you. Angela hasn't done that. She's been honest with you.''

"Carolyn got herself killed because of her wild actions. I just won't let Angela follow in her path. Nor with someone who has the potential for that, either. Mitch said Harry is wild and he's working to teach the kid patience. She doesn't need to be around a kid like that.''

"Ah,'' Laura said and nodded. "Well, then, maybe you're right. But have you told Angela this?''

"You think she'd listen?'' he said and she heard the despair and disbelief in his voice.

"Perhaps, perhaps not. But being honest is important, Zach. You're worried about her getting hurt. Why not level with her?''

"The way she is right now, Laura, she'd just take off running for trouble. She is determined to be wild. She yearns to be like her mother.''

Laura stroked his back before releasing him and stepping back. "She might just have to learn on her own then, that being wild isn't what it's cut out to be. And all you might be able to do is pray God's will be done.''

Zach shook his head stubbornly. "I can protect her. If I try hard enough, keep her out of the things she shouldn't be in."

Laura listened and heard the determination in his voice. She worried that Zach might just find out he couldn't. However, greater miracles had happened and she prayed for both their sakes that they worked it out. "What do you say we all just go to the dance and do our best to enjoy it? You can watch them interact. See how it goes. Then if he seems okay, you can talk to Angela later and tell her she can go, or you can tell her no. That way he isn't coming here to pick her up on a date nor is he bringing her home, and she's under your observation the entire time."

He didn't like it, she could tell that. But he nodded.

"Good. Let's go find Angela."

Zach sighed. "Thanks, Laura." He headed out the front door with her.

It took them only minutes to load up the horses into the trailer and then they were on their way. Angela sat in the middle. Laura wasn't sure if she was happy or disgruntled over that. She did find it amusing when Zach slipped his arm behind Angela as they drove and would reach over and poke Laura's shoulder or stroke a finger down her arm with a knowing smile on his face.

And that certainly passed the time because before she realized it, they were in the town of Hill Creek. Then they had to lead out the two horses from the trailer. Zach was going to ride one of Mitch's that he had brought along.

As Laura entered to back the horse out, she wondered again how she'd been conned into this. Face it, Laura, you were bamboozled by a kid and her father who knew you weren't listening.

Jingle Bells snorted.

"Oh, no. We're not going through this again," she muttered. "I've finally learned the truth about you. I've given you human emotions. All I have to do is pretend you're a dumb animal and everything will be fine. Now back up."

Laura was surprised when the horse backed out with no problems. Grabbing up the saddle she began to saddle her.

"How's it going?" Angela asked, walking

up with her beautiful dun all fixed up and ready to ride.

Laura grinned. "Just fine. I think Jingle Bells has finally figured out who is boss."

Angela chuckled. "She's an angel. I just don't know why you've had so much trouble. Oh, look, here comes Daddy!"

Laura looked and couldn't help the sigh that slipped out as he rode up. Vaguely she realized Mitch was there, too, but Laura had eyes only for Zach.

"You about ready to ride?" he asked, his voice low, his eyes on her.

Laura kneed the horse to make sure it wasn't holding in an extra breath, jerked the cinch then nodded. "As ready as I'll ever be."

Laura took the reins, met the eyes of the horse with a warning.

The horse gave her a dose of bad breath.

Laura flinched. "Ugh."

"What?" Angela asked, mounting her own horse.

"Nothing," Laura replied, thinking the horse had a sick sense of timing. With a breath, she slipped her foot into the holder and waited.

Jingle Bells didn't dance off.

Impressed, she nodded and hauled herself up into the saddle, slipping her other foot into the stirrup.

The horse stood perfectly still. Exuberant, she guided it over by Zach, smiling smugly. "Only a matter of time. You were right."

Zach chuckled. "We're the last ones to go, for obvious reasons. Follow me and we'll get in line."

Laura nodded. "There are people everywhere," she said as she rode alongside Zach. "Where did they all come from?"

He grinned and winked. "If you take in all the farms and outlying areas plus the other nearby towns, we probably have about fifteen thousand people here today. This is an annual event. We'll have chili cook-offs and pie-tasting and a fair, and then we'll have dinner and dancing later. The thing is an all-day-and-night affair. It won't finish up until around 2:00 a.m."

"That long?" Laura gaped.

"We don't always stay that long, but yeah.

They even have a big fireworks display. People out here believe roots are important. This town was founded back in 1869. No matter how big or small it's gotten, people come back every year for the annual town dance.''

"It's more than that," Laura muttered.

"It's the town's birthday, actually. But yeah, it's a whole lot more. It's like a huge family reunion. People open up their homes and put people up. Mitch has two families that he grew up with staying with him. Julian couldn't make it this year." Zach's smile faded. "He couldn't get away from school. However, he'll be home soon."

Zach led them over into a line that backed down Main Street. The air was filled with a festive spirit. People walked along the sidewalks, talking and laughing. All the stores were open, the overhangs outside decorated in different colors. The lawn in front of city hall and the sheriff's office was bright green, having been watered all week.

Vendors sold fireworks and cotton candy and stuffed toys. The high school band was lined up, their teacher getting them all ready with last-minute instructions. It was a scene of controlled chaos.

"You do this every year?"

Zach nodded.

Laura shifted on her horse. "It sounds wonderful."

"It is. It's a time of renewing our roots. So, Laura, I think that's the longest you've stayed on Jingle Bells."

She heard the amusement in his voice and smiled. "Perhaps. However, I think the problems are finally solved. I'm glad Angela got me to ride."

"It's meant a lot to her, your allowing her to teach you every day how to ride this horse."

Laura smiled. "It's meant a lot to me to be with her. And I must admit, getting up on the horse and riding is fun, except for the fact this horse has a sick sense of humor."

"Jingle Bells? Humor? Laura, she's just a horse!"

She scowled at his laughter.

"Okay, okay. Whatever you say."

"I'm ready to ride, how about you?" Angela said, pulling her beautiful dun into line.

"Ready and willing," Laura replied.

"Here we go," Zach whispered.

Sure enough the music started up and dancers and unicyclists and flag bearers and the ROTC all marched, group by group, down Main Street, past the city hall, the funeral home, past the gazebo and high school, ending up at the South Town Grocery Store.

As each group marched and the crowd cheered, Laura realized how attractive this life-style was. She had fallen in love with Hill Creek. She wanted to be a part of it, a part of Zach's life, a part of Angela's life. The friendliness and gentleness in the small town was special and she found she didn't want to give it up.

Why did she suddenly feel so empty on the inside? Why did she feel lost, without direction, as if she'd never been part of anything like this before?

It was their turn and Laura lifted the reins, urging Jingle Bells down the street. People cheered and pointed as the horses went by. It was a wonderful feeling of belonging.

"You're doing wonderful, honey," Zach

whispered. "Just keep it up. We'll be done in a few minutes."

Laura grinned. "This is so much fun. I'll have to do this more often," she said back.

She should have known Jingle Bells would object to that. The horse pulled against the reins and suddenly knelt.

Laura squeaked and grabbed on for dear life.

"Laura!" Angela cried alarmed.

Zach turned his horse, reaching for the reins.

Alarm and laughter exploded in the audience as the horse laid down to roll.

"Watch out!" Zach yelled and sawed on his reins.

Laura jumped, leaping outward and regretting the pain she was going to feel when she hit the pavement.

Instead of pavement she met a strong firm body.

Mitch was there, catching her. Where he came from she had no idea. He stumbled backward and fell with her still clutched in his arms.

Laura groaned in embarrassment.

She heard booted feet, shouts, the sounds of harnesses and spurs as people came running. The others on their horses dismounted.

"You okay, ma'am?" Mitch asked.

"The question is, are you, Mitch? That stupid horse. I should have known she had it in for me."

"Well, if you're done enjoying Laura's company, Mitch, why don't you let me help her up?"

The amused tones of Zach's deep voice brought her rolling off Mitch and looking up. And there stood Jingle Bells, by his side, staring too. Her attention riveted on the horse.

Clambering to her feet, she went up to the horse and grabbed the leather straps. "Listen here, you low-down spawn of an Australian rat, I've had it with you. You think you've won. But this is all-out war now. You've had it. Next time I ride you, you'll regret what you did." She said this low, real low, but she got her point across. The horse stared at her and Laura stared back. Jingle Bells flared her nostrils. Laura sneered. The horse snorted. Laura growled low.

Jingle Bells backed up a step.

She grinned meanly. "Remember that."

Releasing the reins, she turned and found Mitch, Zach and Angela all staring open-mouthed at her. Lifting her chin, she said belligerently, "She knows her place now. So I don't want to hear one word."

"Does that mean you're going to get back up on her and ride her?" Angela asked, not looking too sure about the prospect.

"Do I look crazy? I made my point. Jingle Bells understands I won. I don't plan to ever get on that mangy animal again."

Brushing her hands, she grabbed the reins and started off down the street. "Well, come on. Let's go enjoy the day."

She heard the laughter resume as the crowd dispersed. But she ignored them all, chin in the air, wrapping herself in a blanket of dignity as she led the horses down to where they were going to leave them during the party.

She was almost there before she heard Zach, right next to her whisper, "That was one fine show, Laura, dear. But I'm not going to let you get away with hiding your feelings behind that bravado the rest of day. I'm going to teach you what a small town is all about."

Laura looked over at him and her shield fell, allowing him to see her pleasure at his words. "And I look forward to it, Zach."

He paused, reached down, and stroked her cheek before leaning forward and giving her a gentle kiss. "As do I, Laura, as do I."

Chapter Seventeen

"I'd like to know where you learned to shoot," Zach muttered.

Laura laughed, delighted, hugging the huge teddy bear. "Don't feel bad, Zach, I really didn't mean to outshoot you."

Zach shook his head, grinning ruefully. "It's just smarts."

Laura deposited the teddy bear in the truck and then turned back to Zach. "I'm sorry."

She smiled up at him, knowing she looked smug and unable to help herself. "What can I say? I'm competitive, just like you."

"Six times you beat me, woman."

"And I enjoyed every time." Giggling, she

threw her head back. "Today has been so wonderful, Zach. The people are so friendly, outgoing, warm. The games, the music. Everything has been great."

In the distance the band played, the murmur of voices reached them. But there, by the truck, all Laura saw were the stars just appearing, the peacefulness of her surroundings. The wind blew Zach's hair, ruffling it and she wanted to reach up and run her fingers through it.

"I'm glad you think so, Laura mine." He gently dusted a piece of grass off her blue cotton shirt. Nervously, Laura reached out to close and lock the door, trying to look busy though her mind was centered solely on Zach.

The music on the bandstand changed and slowed. Laura turned and smiled. "I've seen Angela dancing half a dozen dances since the music started up. She sure does have a lot of friends, both boys and girls."

"Yeah. She is having a good time. I was worried after our falling out that she wouldn't. However, I haven't seen you dance a single dance, Laura. Why is that? It's not for lack of people asking."

Laura blushed. "I'm just not real sure that, well, how well I can dance."

Zach reached out and slipped a finger under her chin, tilting her head up. Instead of the amusement she thought she'd see, there was understanding. "We're going to take you to a psychologist Monday and find out just why your memory hasn't come back."

"Zach I—"

"No arguments."

Laura opened her mouth, but subsided. "I think I'd like that. I'm ready to remember, Zach. These flashes of *things* have gotten to me lately. I want to know what's going on."

"Well, let's try to stimulate your memory then, shall we?"

Caught off guard by Zach's words, she asked quizzically, "And just how can you do that?"

Grinning, he took her hand. "By finding out just how well you dance."

"No, Zach, I can't go up in front of those people. I'm liable to make a fool of myself."

"Who said anything about going up in front of those people?"

His arms pulled her forward, and she sud-

denly found herself held lightly in his embrace. She could have broken away if she'd
wanted, could have refused again and was
certain Zach would have released her.

But she didn't. Instead, she slipped her
hands to his chest and, after a hesitation, began to follow him as they danced together, on
the edge of the festivities, with music playing
off in the distance.

The gentle brush of his fingers on her
waist, the concern in his voice as he whispered, "It'll be okay. One step at a time,
Laura mine," brought tears to her eyes.

How could she remember and risk losing
this man? She loved him. She wasn't sure
when it happened. But it did. Was it when
she'd awakened to see the strong sure man,
standing so solidly stable, hat in his hands
staring down at her? Or maybe when she'd
seen the absolute shock on his face when the
chickens had taken off in every direction? It
took someone special to make a person want
to laugh in the middle of chaos.

Was it the way he cared so much about his
daughter and truly struggled to give her a
good life and be the best parent, even admit-

ting that he knew he was making mistakes? Or was it one of any other million tiny things he'd done?

Or was it now, when her heart felt part of his, as if God had brought them together to help the other heal and learn over the past few weeks?

She didn't know when, but all she knew was "I love you."

Zach paused, his eyes going dark. "Say it again."

Laura blinked. His hands pulled her closer, and he whispered. "Say it again, Laura. Let me hear it again."

Oh, heavens. She hadn't said it out loud had she?

"Say you love me."

Yes, she had. "I—I—" she stuttered. "I love you, Zach."

He released a huge breath and pulled her into a bone-crushing embrace. "Oh, Laura, Laura, I can't believe..."

He pulled back, cupped her cheek and kissed her long and slow. Laura's heart sang from such a sweet delicious kiss. When he finally released her she could only stare, breathless, knowing she looked like a fool with such a dazed look on her face, but unable to think let alone string together two words after that kiss.

"I love you, Laura," he whispered and pulled her back into a tender embrace. "I love the way you laugh, the way you chastise, the way you make a mess each time you try to help cook—"

"Hey!"

He chuckled. "I love the way you walk, the way your eyes narrow when you think I'm wrong. I love the way you turn every situation back to God. The peace in your heart despite having no memory..."

He trailed off.

"No memory..." She repeated it low. Wrapping her arms around him she held him, trying to absorb his warmth.

"You'll remember, Laura. It's only a matter of time. And then we'll go from there."

"This way." The low hiss of a nearby voice brought their heads around.

"I really shouldn't do this. Daddy will be mad."

Laura felt Zach stiffen. And she knew why.

The voice. It was Angela's. And dread crawled up Laura's spine.

"It's only a kiss. No one will see us out here."

"I'm afraid that's not quite right," Zach said and pulled away from Laura.

"Daddy!" Angela cried out.

Laura watched Zach stalk forward and face Harry. Grabbing Angela's arm, he pushed her behind him. "I told you, Angie, that trust was something earned. This isn't the way to earn it."

Harry moved nervously before finally propping his boot up on the nearby truck and folding his arms arrogantly.

Fear. She felt it as sure as she felt her heart start to race. It crawled up her spine, engulfing her, tightening her muscles, wrapping around her head until her brain felt as if it were going to explode.

Laura couldn't hear the words as a roaring filled her ears. Bright lights, darkness, boots flashed in her mind. The smell of gasoline and then a whoosh.

In pain, Laura cried out and dropped to her

knees, gripping her head. "I was shot," she whispered.

Strong hands caught her, held her, but she didn't respond. Instead, she stayed turned inward as scene after scene unfolded in her mind. "Boots, fire, gun. My head."

Her fingers traced where the bullet had grazed her and left a line of stitches which later left a scar. "Hate, murder. My brother is missing."

Laura sobbed.

"Laura!" Dimly she heard the panic in Zach's voice and tried to pull herself together.

"He's missing. Mark is missing. I have to find him. The sheriff shot me."

Zach gaped, pulling back. She saw the disbelief and shock on his face. "Mitch wouldn't," he said, and there was anger.

"But true," a voice said, and before Laura could register what had happened, Harry's gun was out and Zach was sinking unconscious to the ground from a pistol blow to the side of the head.

Harry pointed his gun at Laura. Only then did she realize the deputy sheriff had his arm around Angela's neck. She was crying, terror shining in her eyes.

"Get in the car, Laura."

Laura eased up, seeing the party only a few hundred yards away, wondering if she should take the chance and yell.

Evidently, Harry read her mind. "Do it and I kill his daughter. I don't have anything to lose. I was supposed to keep an eye on you. They were supposed to check in by now. I don't know where they are. I'm not taking this rap alone. I was going to take Angela for insurance. But both of you would be better than one. Now go."

Laura saw him sweating, registered the banked panic in his eyes and knew, from all the cases she had worked on in the past, the best thing to do was go along with it. "Why don't you let her go? She can't do anything to—"

"I said go!"

Laura cast a look down at Zach as she walked past, praying he was okay. She reached into her pocket for the keys and unlocked the door to the truck.

Harry slipped in, shoving Angela in before

him, keeping the gun trained on Laura. "You had to come searching for your brother. Everything was fine. He got snoopy and he had an 'accident' when he fell off the cliff. Nothing else should have happened. Get in!"

Laura slid in and started the vehicle. Her hands trembled. *Mark, oh Mark,* she cried silently.

"You know someone is going to find out."

Harry slapped her. "Shut up. Just shut up. I gotta think. Drive down the road to the old line shack."

Laura flinched in pain but did as he said, pulling the door closed and driving off, never looking back. She had to think of something. If Harry killed her brother and then told her, he wasn't going to let them live. If she could only get Angela out of the car. But Harry now had the gun turned on Laura at her neck. One wrong action and as spooked as he was, he'd pull the trigger.

"So, what was it you were into, Harry? You and your friends? This part of Texas I'd guess illegal aliens."

Harry laughed nastily. "No, man. They're into smuggling drugs. I got paid to look the other way. I took patrol on the nights they were going to be out and gave Mitch the night free. Was a nice bit of extra money. Being deputy doesn't pay enough.''

Angela whimpered and Laura's grip on the wheel tightened as they drove. "It was you who set my car on fire and shot me that night, wasn't it?''

"Some old coot called the station and asked if there was a hotel in the area and could we make reservations for a woman who was looking for her brother. After your brother found out, they didn't want anyone else snooping around. So, I took care of it. Took an old truck from the junkyard at old man Byer's place. He's a drunk and never would notice it missing.''

"I see,'' she said, shaking with the effort to suppress all of her emotions as her mind raced to find an escape. "So, my brother was simply an accident? He stumbled onto something he shouldn't have and had to pay the price.''

"It wasn't supposed to be like this,'' Harry muttered. "Here, turn off here.'' He pointed to a dirt road that led out into the desert.

"This was the last run they were going to make. You screwed it all up. They thought it better to get a different route to be on the safe side. I have a feeling Mitch was getting wise. Thought if his niece came up missing, that'd distract from what had been going on. Then you had to get your memory back."

The gun lowered, scraping her neck as she hit a bump. "Why couldn't you have just stayed away?"

"You really don't think the men behind this operation are going to take you with them, do you, Harry? They use kids like you all the time. They give you hope of a better life, of a path to follow for quick easy money, and then when the heat comes, they disappear into the night, leaving the kids to take the heat. Kids get shorter sentences and are a dime a dozen."

"I said shut up!"

He hit Laura again, and Angela started sobbing. Laura sucked in a sharp breath as she saw stars. "Smart, Harry. Trying to get us killed?"

"There it is!"

Sure enough, in the distance was a small

one-room shack that looked like it was falling apart.

Laura stopped and concentrated as she was pushed out of the truck. Harry kept his distance, the gun on Angela as he motioned them forward.

Meeting Angela's eyes, Laura tried to reassure her. *Father, help us. I'm out of ideas on this one,* she silently prayed.

"Go on in."

Laura didn't want to go in. Once inside, she was certain their chances decreased. Anything was better than going in that door. Yet, what choice did she have? Sighing, she went inside. Harry shoved Angela in and slammed the door.

Laura was knocked to her knees by the impact of the door but immediately turned and gathered Angela in her arms. Harry was on the other side of the door. "Come on," she whispered jumping to her feet.

Harry jerked the door open, lantern in one hand and gun in the other. "Stay there!"

So, he was getting a light. Laura pulled Angela up next to her and eased in front of the young girl.

"Laura," Angela whispered, whimpering.

"Move." Harry motioned them apart.

Slowly, Laura shook her head. "I'm sorry, Harry. I love Angela and I love her father. I can't move and put her in danger."

Laura felt Angela start to move to her side. "No, Angie. Stay behind me."

"But he's gonna shoot you," Angela said, her breathing short, harsh as she tried to stop her tears.

Laura edged back away from Harry. "If he does, he does. But I don't think he wants to shoot us. I think he wants to talk and wait for his buddies."

Laura knew better. The young man looked wild-eyed, only a hairbreadth from panic.

"If you don't move, I swear I'm gonna…"

The door burst inward hitting Harry.

Harry went flying and Zach, looking a bit worse for wear, flew after him.

Laura whirled and shoved Angela toward the door, herding her. "Out, now Angie."

"Don't move!"

Harry still had the gun pointed at Angie.

Laura saw the desperation in his eyes, knew he realized he couldn't win and was going to do as much damage as possible be-fore the end. "No!" she yelled and threw herself at Angela, wrapping her arms around her just as the gun went off.

Oh, man, she thought when the dull impact hit her in the shoulder, throwing her hard against Angela and sending them both to the floor. I've felt this before. *Pain. Pain. Pain.* Her mind filled with it.

She heard Zach's cry of rage and then the sound of a scuffle. Angela was weeping, beg-ging her not to die. Groggily, Laura whis-pered, "I'm not going to. Get out, go for help."

"DEA. Stay where you are."

Laura heard the shout. "Never mind," she whispered, and the world turned black.

Chapter Eighteen

"Laura? Laura Walker?"

Laura blinked and opened her eyes, to see one of the most gorgeous doctors she'd ever seen looking down at her, penlight in his hand. "Oh," she whispered, meeting the dark laughing eyes that seemed so familiar. "Do I know you?'

He chuckled. "Not amnesia again, I hope."

"No. I...Angela, Zach. Are they okay?"

"They're just fine." He stepped aside and Laura saw them by the door. With a cry, Angela rushed forward and threw herself onto Laura, hugging her.

"I thought you were going to die," she said.

Laura winced, but wrapped her arms around Angela, being careful of the IV in her hand.

"Laura, honey, meet my other brother, Julian McCade."

"That's why you look familiar," she said.

"That's one thing about the McCades. We all look the same."

Turning, she saw Mitch on the other side of her bed. "What happened?"

Zach couldn't restrain himself any longer. He moved forward and dropped down on the edge of the bed and lifted her hand to his lips. "You were shot."

"Here we go again," Mitch murmured, amusement rife in his words.

Zach shot him a look. "That's enough."

"No, I mean...how did I get here?"

You took a bullet meant for Angie."

"I know. I know." She shook her head. "I...I remember the DEA."

Julian smiled and slipped an arm around Angela. "Give her room, kid. Let's give your dad room and let your uncle Mitch explain."

Angela hugged Julian and stood aside.

Laura was certain she was Dorothy and she wasn't in Kansas anymore. "Okay, wait. Let me start. I got my memory back. Harry's boots. He shot me." Laura lifted a hand and touched her head. "They killed…my brother."

Zach pulled her into his arms. "I'm sorry. Oh, honey."

"Oh, Zach," she whispered and hugged him tightly, grief filling her.

"The DEA came in," Zach whispered, his voice running through her, encouraging her. "Evidently they had some information on a drug-smuggling ring and had been watching the sheriff's department as well as me. It seems their witness thought we were in on it. Last night they were making a run and the DEA moved in. They came to the old shack planning to get the drugs stored there and meet and clean up anyone left."

"How'd you get there, Zach?"

"I came to just as you were driving off. I managed to get in the tail end of the truck."

"Thank you," Laura whispered. "I may be

a homicide detective but something like that I could never handle by myself.''

Realizing what she said, she looked up at Zach. "Your wife. Oh, Zach, I'm sorry. I'm not like her.''

"I know that, honey. I know that. Carolyn was reckless. You never have been.''

"I love you, Zach,'' she said, and tears slipped down her face. "I love you so much.''

"And I love you, Laura mine. So much.''

Angela broke free from Julian and moved up to Laura, reminding her they had an audience. Sobbing softly, Angela hugged her daddy. "I'm sorry, Daddy. I love you and I love Laurie, too. I should have listened to you both.''

Zach turned, pulling his daughter into his arms. "It's okay, sweetie. We've both learned from this. I'll try harder to be more understanding.''

"And I promise to listen to you.''

Laura cried with joy.

"So, are you going to marry her, Daddy?'' Angela asked.

Mitch coughed and turned his back, walking over toward the window. Julian chuckled, then covered his mouth trying to wipe the smirk away. Zach looked dumbfounded then looked at Laura, who was certain she didn't look much better. "I—I, well," he shook his head. "This wasn't how I planned it, but yeah. Laura, I think God sent you here just for my family, to bring healing and renewal. I never thought I'd find love again, but I guess sometimes God has other plans. Will you marry me, be a friend to my daughter, and a lover and wife and a friend to me?"

Laura smiled softly. "Oh, Zach..."

Choked up, she didn't think she could answer as fresh tears ran down her face. "Well, Laurie. You gonna answer him?"

The voice from near the door jerked her head around. An old Indian, a DEA officer and a young man on crutches stood there. "Mark!" she cried.

The young man grinned.

"But you're dead! Oh, Mark!"

"Your brother?"

All three brothers turned to stare at her battered, bruised, but alive brother in the doorway.

"They had to keep me under wraps, let the gang believe I was dead. I'm sorry I couldn't let you know I was alive, Sis. When I went over the cliff, it was decided, after Will found me and we called the DEA, to keep my identity a secret since we weren't sure who was in on the drug dealing."

Looking at Zach, her brother offered an apologetic nod. "Sorry, Mr. McCade."

Mark hobbled across the room and hugged her close.

Laura cried and cried and cried.

"Hey now, Sis. You, ever strong, crying all over me. You're embarrassing me," he whispered, though she heard the love and concern in her voice.

Finally releasing him, she wiped at her face. "I had to find you, Mark. I've neglected you and so many things while trying to fulfill some stupid dream that really isn't all that important."

Mark smiled. "You've finally found your path," he said softly.

"Yes."

"So, are you going to answer the man?" Mark asked.

"Oh!" She looked back over to Zach, who was still sitting patiently by her holding her hand.

"Well, Laura?" he asked quietly. "Can you give up the big city and live out here?"

"I can give up anything for you," she replied. "Yes. Yes, yes, yes, I want to marry you."

She tugged him down to her and wrapped an arm around him. Zach didn't settle for that though as he turned his head and kissed her. She heard the brothers hoot with laughter and make some silly remarks but she didn't care. She returned the kiss, happier than she could remember.

"Ahem," Mitch said, breaking them apart. "Actually, if Laura wants a job, I have an opening for a deputy sheriff that she is more than qualified for."

"Really?"

She looked at Zach.

"I can't think of anything better suited for you, love."

"Thank you, Zach," she whispered and leaned up, kissing him again gently.

Finally, she turned to the one person in the

room who had been so quiet. "Is this okay with you, Angie? Would you mind your daddy marrying me?"

Angela hesitated then asked, "Do I have to call you Mom?"

Gently, Laura pulled her down by her, dislodging Zach's hold. "No, sweetie, you don't. You can call me whatever you want. I imagine we'll just have to take the relationship one day at a time if you agree. But right now, I think we have a good start. I consider you a dear friend."

Tears slipped down Angela's cheeks. "I love you, Laurie."

"And I you, sweetie."

"You don't have to ride Jingle Bells anymore."

Laura laughed. "I think Jingle Bells and I have come to an agreement."

"Jingle Bells?" Mark asked.

"A horse," Zach replied.

"You got my sister on a horse?" Her brother sounded incredulous.

She ignored her brother. "One day at a time, Angie. But it's up to you."

Angela hugged her and then said, "I'd be

real happy if you'd marry my daddy, Laurie.'' Angela turned and hugged her father again.

"Then it's settled."

"You may have to worry, big brother. Both of them agreeing. I can see troublesome times ahead for you," Julian said.

Zach smiled down at Laura. "In this case I have no arguments."

Laura squeezed his hand and realized only a year ago her one desire was to fulfill a dream made from sand castles. Now though, she'd found her true direction, and all because a man had thought her his daughter's nanny.

"I guess sometimes God has to knock us completely down, my love, in order to guide us, doesn't he?" she whispered.

Leaning down, he whispered back, "But he always helps us back up."

Quietly the others left the room, allowing Laura and Zach to discuss their new future and their new ready-made family.

*   *   *   *   *

If you enjoyed reading
For Love of Zach
you'll love FOR LOVE OF HAWK,
the second book in
Cheryl Wolverton's
HILL CREEK, TEXAS *series.*

For a sample of
FOR LOVE OF HAWK,
just turn the page....

Chapter One

‎

"This is where you're going to set up practice?"

Julian McCade winced when his big brother, Zach, the head of their family, kicked at a beat-up wastepaper basket on the floor. Julian had to admit it looked bad. The ancient clinic had definitely fallen into disrepair, looking more like a broken-down house of fifty years rather than a clinic which had only been empty five. "The dingy walls need a good painting, and the stale white cabinets and countertops need a good reworkin—"

"Not to mention the tiled floor," Mitch, his middle brother and sheriff of their hometown said as he toed a loose tile with his booted foot.

Julian looked from one brother to the other. It was obvious from their tan skin and dark hair, the square shape of the jaw and even from their lean builds, that these men were his brothers.

The difference? His oldest brother, Zach, had blue eyes unlike his own brown ones.

"This is better than using the former doctor's office. You know a lot of people from the outlying ranches and the poor had trouble getting into town where he lived. We have to go where the people are. That's why the hospital is begging for someone to reopen this clinic."

Julian felt five years old again, with both of his big brothers getting to him.

Zach, at thirty-six, stood tall and steady, his gaze traveling around the room as he took in the disaster area before him. Dark gritty walls from years of disuse faced them in the kitchen of the old Fullerton Clinic. Wallpaper that had once graced the walls now hung in loose strips.

The long wing right off the kitchen that

was the actual clinic was in a bit better shape. Still, Julian didn't like admitting Zach had a point. The kitchen was a mess. Evidently, drifters had made free use of it. If he could clean this and the waiting room up, he'd have a place for patients to wait and for him to cook. The house had three small rooms set up as living quarters for whoever ran the clinic.

Zach snorted and shifted. His hands slipped into his jeans pockets, his hat tipped lazily back on his head. Zach was firm, and it was next to impossible to get a point through to him. That was one reason why he now turned to Mitch, hoping for help. He should have known better.

Mitch, in his tan sheriff's uniform and hat in hand, looked downright belligerent.

"We just busted a drug gang, Julian. You don't need to be out here alone—"

"The hospital is hiring a partner," Julian pointed out patiently, having learned not to get ornery with his brothers—especially when they were both on the same side.

"I think it's wonderful that you'll be out here for them."

Laura. The last occupant of the room. Julian glanced over at the willowy blond woman and smiled. Out of everyone here, she had been on his side backing him up since he had returned to the area two weeks ago. His sister-in-law understood the necessity to move farther out into the wilderness after nearly losing her brother out here.

She also had backed Julian when both brothers had wanted him living out at the old homestead instead of here. Laura had informed them that as an adult on his own for several semesters now, he might have other ideas about just where he wanted to live. When she had backed him after his brothers had immediately nixed the idea of his opening the run-down clinic, he had decided he really liked his sister-in-law.

She had actually challenged Zach and gotten him to agree to come out and at least look at the place.

And now, the way Zach was looking at his wife, Julian realized Laura just might succeed in getting his oldest brother off his back. Things here in Hill Creek had certainly changed since he'd been away at medical school.

"Well, my deputy might be able to talk you into agreeing, Zach." Mitch's voice intruded into Julian's thoughts. "But she isn't going to be changing my mind." Mitch turned his dark eyes from Zach to Julian and frowned severely. "Jul, the place out here is dangerous. This is the very property the DEA caught the drug smugglers on, the same ones who almost murdered your sister-in-law."

"As I heard it," Julian said, coolly, "it was your old deputy that did that."

Mitch bristled.

Laura interrupted. "You're right. It was Harry who shot me. However, Julian, that's not the point. The point is, your brothers are simply worried about you. How about a compromise?"

Both Zach and Mitch looked warily at Laura. Julian didn't care that they stared at her as if she'd suddenly called fire down on them. He grabbed the chance to get both brothers off his back. "What type of compromise?" he encouraged Laura.

"You let your brothers and friends fix up the kitchen and private quarters, let them have the phone turned on, the tanks filled and everything that will make basic survival out here safe. Then they'll back off and allow you to do what you want.''

Julian glared. She was on his side? He didn't think so. That plan might make sense to someone else. But not him.

Now he knew why his brothers had stared at Laura like that. He didn't want to depend on his brothers at all. He had no desire to let them interfere in anything he did. He wanted to prove to them he could do it all. He wasn't going to let them meddle.

Of course, he wasn't a bit surprised when *they* liked the idea.

''Sounds good to me,'' Zach said, smiling at his wife. When had Zach gone so soft? Julian wondered.

''I still don't like it,'' Mitch muttered.

Zach gave Mitch the superior I'm-the-oldest look.

''But I'll go along with it,'' Mitch agreed reluctantly.

''Well, I hate to disappoint you, but I won't,'' Julian said, interrupting their mutual agreements.

''What?'' all three said in unison, turning

to stare at him. Laura looked shocked. Zach stared with an inscrutable look. And Mitch, well, Mitch scowled as if he were angry again.

Taking a deep breath, Julian forged ahead with what he hadn't told them before, the news that would really upset them. "I've already talked to the hospital and I've talked with the bank. The hospital thinks the site is ideal and the bank has loaned me enough money to get me started."

Zach frowned, his features darkening. "You've already decided? Before you even got us out here?"

"It was my decision," Julian said firmly. Man, he thought, facing down a gang intent on getting to one of his patients was easier than facing his two brothers.

"It's not just *your* decision but *our* decision," Zach said low. "What you do affects this family. We should have at least been consulted."

"I'm fully grown, I don't have to consult you on what I do."

Laura glanced between the brothers. "Let's all just calm down."

Zach paused then nodded. "Fine. I'll be at the ranch if he comes to his senses."

"You'll be at the ranch a long time then," Julian retorted.

Mitch shook his head and stalked off after his older brother.

Laura sighed and gave Julian one of those looks totally reserved for a five-year-old who has done something bad and knows it. At least she didn't shake her finger, though the way she shook her head made him wonder if that meant the same thing. "Be good, Julian. Now I have to go handle a bear. He only loves you."

"Well, he doesn't have to smother me," he told Laura, again feeling frustrated and angry at his older brothers and not sure why.

Laura's frown faded and she moved forward, laying a gentle hand on Julian's tan stretchy top. She squeezed his upper arm slightly, her eyes asking him to understand, to listen. "Be glad you have someone who cares."

Julian lifted his other hand and placed it over her smaller one, his dark skin making hers look all that much lighter. He liked his sister-in-law. She was gentle, tender, caring. He didn't know anyone like that. She really cared about Zach and Mitch and even him. Her next words confirmed just how much her new family meant to her. "Don't let it end like this. The Bible tells us not to let the sun set on our wrath."

Julian gave in. Who wouldn't, when someone like Laura gave him such an entreating look? With a reluctant nod, he acquiesced. "Very well."

Laura's face glowed like a brightly lighted Christmas tree on a cold dark night.

No wonder Zach couldn't resist Laura. Julian was certainly glad this woman wasn't his problem. He had a feeling he'd give her whatever she asked, too. "Okay, okay. Turn off the joy, Laura. I'm doing it."

She hugged him, chuckling, and then stepped back. "You catch on faster than Mitch, but don't tell him I said that." She winked.

Julian simply shook his head before sprinting out the door. He easily spotted Zach. In the overgrown dirt parking lot, there were only two vehicles besides his. Zach's dusty forest-green truck and Mitch's four-by-four that was black and brown and sitting next to his sporty red hatchback. "Hey, Zach, wait."

Zach paused at the truck, his gaze cutting back to Julian. "Yeah?"

"Look," Julian began. He didn't want to give in, but he also didn't want strife between them. Since Zach had raised them after their parents had been killed in a freak skydiving accident, Zach was more than just a brother. Zach was the foundation of a world turned topsy-turvy. When they could have been broken up and sent to different homes, at nineteen Zach fought to keep the family together, to keep them all in church and to keep them all at home.

"Don't leave angry," Julian said. And meant it this time.

Zach had succeeded in keeping them together and Julian admired and loved his brother for that. But Julian had no desire to stay here—especially if it meant staying here and facing the family rift that he caused.

"I have a debt to pay to the county hospital. I signed that agreement with them when they let me work my last year of high school training there with their doctors in that special jump-start program. You know that. And you know I'll be here two years.''

He'd promised the hospital five years of service or two years in a branch clinic that he would run if his grades were high. He'd graduated fifteenth in his class of five hundred. So, he had two years of service he owed Hill Creek County Memorial Hospital before his debt was considered paid and he could move on to greener pastures.

"I simply want to fulfill my contract. And a clinic is the best way to do that. You know we need it." Two years would also be long enough to show his brothers he didn't need their help every time he made a decision. Then he'd be off to chase his dream.

"Two years before you leave," Zach muttered.

"Two years he'll be with us," Laura corrected from behind Julian before walking over and slipping an arm through Zach's and smiling sweetly up at him.

"Will you stop that?" Mitch drawled, the heat gone from his voice and the good humor restored. "You know he can't think when you look at him like that."

"Yeah, I do." Laura grinned smugly and squeezed Zach's arm.

Zach's frown eased into a soft smile and he chuckled. "Not true," he murmured.

"But it *is* true your brother is back. He'll be here for two years. And fighting isn't the way God wants you to start out Julian's return."

Zach leaned down and kissed her on the tip of her nose. "You're right, sweetheart." Shifting his weight, he pivoted toward Julian. "I apologize, Julian, for my attitude. We want you back and..." As if realizing going any further would only start the argument back, he hesitated.

"And," Laura interjected, "we'll be glad to support you in this project. Right?"

Zach tipped his hat back and looked up at the sky. "Women."

"You married her." Mitch's voice rang with amusement.

"You hired her," Zach retorted. "Okay, okay. Of course we'll support you. You know that. We'd just like to know what's going on with you, not find out after the fact. How would you feel if the hospital hired a partner for you and didn't tell you until that partner arrived? You'd be frustrated, upset, angry, wouldn't you?''

Slowly, Julian shook his head. ''Not at all. Why do you think that? A partner is a partner. Why would I care, as long as the doctor was a good doctor? And to work out here, the hospital wants only the top graduates. So, I have nothing to worry about.''

''Give it up, big bro.'' Mitch shook his head and started toward his four-by-four. ''He's not going to give in.''

''Well, that's just how we felt,'' Zach continued, ignoring Mitch's advice. Julian watched the way Zach slipped his arm around Laura, so casually, absently, pulling her up against his side and squeezing her. He silently thanked God that Zach had finally found someone.

''Hey, someone's coming this way,'' Mitch interrupted, pointing toward a dust cloud in the distance on the driveway that led out to the ranch—a driveway that was nearly forty-five minutes long.

Julian lifted a hand, shielding his eyes against the midday glare of the winter sun. Sure enough, someone certainly was headed toward them. As the car got closer he saw it was a beat-up old Volkswagen Bug, gunmetal gray, the paint having worn off a long time before.

Why did that car seem vaguely familiar and cause a feeling of dread to work its way up his spine? he wondered.

"Wonder who it is?" Zach murmured as the car came closer.

"Not from around here. I'd know the car," Mitch replied.

"Oh, no," Julian suddenly whispered. *No, no no.* It couldn't be. He took two steps forward toward the vehicle that turned into the parking lot. The dust swirled up around the car, but not enough to block the bright-red curls that bounced as the woman twisted the wheel and came to an abrupt stop next to him.

He was close enough to see her eyes, those deep-green eyes he'd thought—hoped—to never see again. Then she grinned, that bright infectious grin that lured every person in, encouraged them to be at ease, until she went for the kill.

"She seems to know you," Laura said as she started forward.

He wanted to warn Laura to stay back, to leave, find somewhere else to go, but it was too late. With a huge grin she waved, and shoved open the door.

And hit Julian right square below the belt. "Oooaf."

He heard his own groan, felt the waves of pain as he sank to the ground. Both brothers shouted and started forward, but he ignored them. Through the haze of pain, he saw the familiar wince as the woman jumped out of the car, and then, heard her cry, "Hawk! Oh, dear, I didn't mean that."

Julian sank the rest of the way to the ground and smiled through a tight face. "Of course you didn't, Freckles."

"You know her?" Zach asked and it was nice to hear the note of wariness in his voice, see the look of pity in his eyes.

Before he could answer though, the woman came forward. "Oh, yes. Hawk and I know each other well. I'm a doctor. Let me through. I'll see if he's oka-a-a-ay—''

Julian managed to get his arms up just in time to catch the woman as she tripped and landed on top of him.

He saw stars as their heads collided.

She gasped and then grabbed his shoulders.

Blinking, he looked up at her. "Susan. What brings you here?''

She reached up and rubbed her forehead before answering. "Surprise. I'm your new partner.''

Somehow, he'd just known she was going to say that.